Ken and Jesse met as new next-door neighbors when they were very young. They grew up together and were best friends. As time passed, they became even closer. The realization that Ken meant more to Jesse than just friendship came to a head at a party celebrating their birthdays.

Jesse was drinking heavily and started getting jealous about the attention Ken was getting from Jesse's buddies. An argument ensued, and Ken was severely beaten by Jesse and his friends.

Ken spent many days in the hospital, and his recovery was painful for everyone, especially for Jesse.

Jesse attempted suicide but failed. Ken snuck into the hospital and said to Jesse, "Please live because I can't be in this world without you in it."

Jesse moved to another university. He studied hard and became a doctor. He never stopped loving Ken.

Ken stayed in his hometown. Long ago, he'd forgiven Jesse. It was time for them both to move on and let the past go. They reunited when Jesse came home for Christmas.

They have some struggles, but the love they always had flourishes.

Trigger warning: Suicide attempt.

Perfect Love Never Ends
Copyright © 2024 James J Gregoryk
ISBN: 978-1-4874-4133-3
Cover art by Martine Jardin

Published by eXtasy Books Inc

Look for us online at:
www.eXtasybooks.com

Perfect Love Never Ends

By

James J Gregoryk

DEDICATION

I am so grateful for my friends and family, who have lovingly supported my writing endeavors. I dedicate this story in the loving memory of my parents, Metka and Robert Hansen. I thank Helen and David for their loving care and encouragement.

CHAPTER ONE

Jesse and Kenny were best friends since the day Kenny's family moved next door. Kenny was four, and Jesse was five. They were inseparable since the day they met twenty-three years ago.

"Hi, I'm Jesse. Who are you?"

"Kenny."

"Hi Kenny, I have been waiting for you for a long time."

Kenny's mother panicked a little when Jesse reached over the garden fence and picked Kenny up.

"Let's go play." They ran off into Jesse's backyard. Kenny's father needed to stop his overly protective mother from running them down and taking her son back.

Kenny's grandma called them the giant and the elf, as Jesse was always two heads taller than Kenny. The two of them did everything together.

Kenny went to all of Jesse's sports activities. In turn, Jesse went to all of Kenny's music recitals. Kenny's parents, Paul and Nanette Van Dever, and Jesse's parents, Janie and Barry Hanover, became great friends, too. They were like one big family. The families celebrated everything together. The birth of Jesse's sister, Carrie Ann, and Kenny's baby brother, Bobby, only added to their happiness.

The boys were inseparable, and everyone knew it throughout the school. When Jesse went to high school, it was hard for Kenny to be separated from Jesse, but there was no choice. Still, Jesse met him at middle school at the end of the day, and they walked home together.

The most challenging time came when Jesse went off to the university. He wanted to stay home and work a year so he and Kenny could go together, but his parents would have none of that stuff. Jesse left, and Kenny cried for days. Jesse proved to be a great friend and called Ken every day and came home often.

It was a very lonely year for Kenny. He missed sharing every little thing with Jesse. Jesse came home to celebrate their birthdays. Their birthdays fell on the same day, and they spent the entire day together. Jesse turned nineteen, and Kenny eighteen. That was the day they pledged to be best friends forever.

Everything changed on their twenty-first and twenty-second birthdays. Jesse convinced Kenny that they needed to go out with his football buddies and really celebrate. Even though Kenny didn't like the idea much, Jesse talked him into going to the *Players Bar and Grill.*

It was fun at first — a little beer — a little food — some more beer, and then some birthday cake. Jesse drank more beer and then even more. One of Jesse's friends, Randy, started flirting with Kenny. Sara, Kenny's best friend, laughed and teased him about it.

Jesse started to get very loud and aggressive toward everyone, but especially toward Kenny.

He begged Kenny to play pool with the guys. Reluctantly, Kenny joined them.

Jesse started ridiculing him, "You are such a wuss. You did that like a girl. What are you, some sort of homo? God, what a total fag you are!"

Kenny finally had enough and flung the cue stick onto the table. "Fuck you, asshole. Happy Birthday to us." He stormed out of the bar to where he'd parked his car.

He reached for the door handle, but someone grabbed his

shirt from behind and yanked him away from the car. It was Jesse, and he was like a crazy man. "You fucking little faggot, don't you ever fucking do that to me again, embarrass me in front of my best friends."

He slapped Kenny so hard that it knocked him down, and the back of his head hit the car as he fell.

Jesse's teammates had gathered around and started taunting him to *kick the shit out of that fag.* Drunk, angry, and out of his mind, Jesse backed away. He stood there, unable to move. The others started kicking Kenny. Curling up into a ball, Kenny tried to protect himself as much as possible.

There was a loud *whack,* and one of the players went down.

Sara, holding a large branch, screamed, "You all are fucking killing him. Jesse, it's Ken! Have you all gone berserk or what? Why are you just standing here? My God, I think he may be dying! Call nine-one-one!"

The boys stopped and looked down at Kenny. One of them said, "Holy shit, I'm out of here." They all scattered, including Jesse, leaving Kenny there to die.

Sara would have none of that. "You better not even fucking think of dying on me, Kenny, I need you."

The ambulance and police cars arrived at the same time. Sara frantically told them what had happened. They loaded Kenny and were off with sirens blaring. The police officers were very kind and gentle with Sara. They took her to the station, where she called Kenny's parents and told them what had happened.

Kenny's parents repeatedly asked, "Jesse did that to Kenny? Why would he do this?"

Sara was so upset all she could answer was, "I don't know." Sara's mother came and took the pathetic shaken girl home.

Kenny's parents called Jesse's parents and filled them in about what Sara told them about their sons.

"Oh my God, what can we do?" Jesse's mom asked.

"Pray." Kenny's dad told them, and his parents rushed off to the hospital.

Kenny's parents were met at the entrance to the emergency room by one of the doctors treating Kenny.

"He's in pretty bad shape right now. We know he has a broken nose, eye socket, several knocked-out teeth, a fractured arm, and six fractured ribs. His leg muscles and tendons are severely damaged. He's unconscious and unresponsive. Kenny's currently getting a CT scan to see if there are any internal injuries or brain damage."

"I need to see my baby," Kenny's mother said. She was on the verge of breaking down; her hands trembled, and her eyes filled with tears.

The doctor took her hands. "I promise you, the moment we can get him into the ICU, you can see him."

Kenny's parents both nodded.

An hour later, a nurse came to get the Van Devers. She described what they would be seeing when they saw their son. "I want you both to understand. Right now, he doesn't look like himself at all. He's bruised and swollen. It'll be a shock for you to see him. I know this will be very hard for you both, but I need you to stay calm and quiet, or the staff will escort you back to the waiting room. Our psychologist is waiting for you just outside of Kenny's room. She'll help you get through this. Okay, are you ready?"

The Van Devers both nodded.

Seeing their son in that condition horrified them. Kenny's mom could only say, "Oh my God," over and over again. They sat on the chairs beside the bed and touched their son as the nurse described Kenny's condition.

Over the next couple of days, Kenny's parents took turns being with him. They washed and talked to him.

Jesse's parents came to the hospital and sat and talked to the Van Devers. They couldn't comprehend how their son could have done such a terrible thing. They apologized over and over again.

Kenny's dad finally said, "You're our closest and dearest friends. We both know you love Kenny. We'll get through this. Thank you for coming. I know this was a hard thing for you to do. Have you talked with Jesse? Does he have a reason for this happening?"

Mr. Hanover said, "We don't know where he is. No one has seen him. The cops are looking for him everywhere."

The couples hugged, and the Hanovers left.

Kenny's dad looked at his wife. "I can't imagine the hell they must be going through."

She looked up at him. "Not nearly close to the hell that we're going through."

Kenny woke up four days later with his head bandaged, his arm in a cast, and his right leg lifted off the bed. Looking around, he realized he was in the hospital. He looked at his mother, sleeping in a chair with her head on the bed. He tried to talk, but something was in his throat. He started to fight to get it out.

"Oh my God, you're awake!" She pressed the call button. "Nurse, please help! He's awake!" His mother tried to keep his hand off the tubes. Several nurses appeared. They held him down, someone put something into the IV, and he was out. Kenny was in and out of consciousness for the next day. They kept him that way until he was stable enough to understand what was happening to him. After they removed the breathing tube, he was moved to a regular room.

When he woke up the next morning, his mom, dad, brother Bobby and Sara stared at him. His mom and dad burst into tears, and Bobby grabbed his hand and kissed it. "Welcome back, big brother."

Sara said, "Here." She then put something cold into his mouth, ice chips. They felt so good. He opened his mouth like a baby bird, and she kept them coming.

Finally, when he could talk, Kenny said, "Why?"

Mom responded, "Why are you here, honey? Because you were severely beaten six days ago, you're in the hospital."

"No, why?" Kenny started to cry, partly due to the pain that was welling up and partly due to the question he needed answered.

"Why what, son," Dad asked.

Tears flowed. "Why did they do this to me?"

Everyone froze. Finally, Sara said, "We don't know, my dear friend, we just don't know. No one has seen Jesse."

His mother became a ferocious beast suddenly. "I hope he rots in jail along with the other bastards that did this to you!"

Kenny turned to his dad. "No jail, Dad, no jail. I won't press charges. Dad, you know why and what to do."

Dad nodded, took his near frantic mother by the hand, and took her out to explain everything to her.

Bobby looked so puzzled.

Kenny responded, "Bobby, I love Jesse. Even after he did this, I still love him. I'll probably never forgive him, but I can't stop loving him. He's part of my soul."

Kenny's mom stormed into the room. "Here." Holding up a mirror. "This is what the great love of your life did to you."

Kenny didn't recognize the person he saw.

"He and his wonderful friends broke your nose, eye socket, knocked out teeth, broke your arm, and six ribs, plus you may have nerve damage to your spine, permanent leg damage, and he caused you to have swelling on the brain. We're still unsure if there is neurological damage and you nearly died. And you're going to just let him go? Is that what you're saying?"

"Mom, you and Dad taught us about unconditional love, and I do love him. I can't forgive him for what he did, but I still love him so much. Mom, I'll heal and be fine, but I doubt Jesse will ever be."

Dad shuffled everyone out. He smiled at Kenny, who mouthed a thanks to his dad. Kenny needed time to think and rest.

Kenny awoke to see Jesse standing at the door to Kenny's room, watching him, crying. His clothes looked dirty and like he hadn't changed in days. He saw the anguish on Jesse's face. He actually felt it. "Jesse, get out and don't come back. I want you never to try to see me again. I'll never understand why you all did this. Never bother me again, now go. I love you, but go."

Jesse stood there silently, sobbing. He couldn't speak; he tried, but there were no words. He opened and closed his mouth several times.

"Go, Jesse, just go."

Defeated, Jesse dropped his head and started to turn. Without looking at Kenny, he said, "I'm so sorry. I love you, Kenny, more than you will ever know. I wish I were dead." He fled away.

Jesse wandered around. He tried not to be found. He ate nothing and drank very little. The cops finally found him in the park, sitting on a swing.

"Jesse Hanover? Are you Jesse Hanover?"

Jesse looked up and said, "I hurt my best friend. The person I love most in the world. He's broken because of me."

One of the cops spoke softly to him. "Jesse, your mom and dad are sick with worry. Can we take you home?"

"You mean jail."

"No, son, not jail. Home. Kenny Van Dever refused to press charges. We want to take you to your parents."

"My parents don't want me. They hate me for what I've done." Jesse covered his face and sobbed.

"Listen to me. Son, they've been searching for you for six days. They're frantic to get you home. Come on, let's go."

They loaded Jesse into their patrol car and drove him home. The officers walked Jesse to his parents' front door and knocked. Jesse's dad opened the door, took one look, and pulled his son into his arms, hugging him tightly. He shouted, "Janie, our boy is home."

An anguished cry sounded from behind them. The sound of running feet came toward them. "My baby, you're safe." His mother cried and joined the hug. After a few minutes, Jesse's dad let go and then thanked the police officers, and they left.

"Mom and Dad, I hurt Kenny. How can you even want me around? I'm a terrible person. I don't belong in this family of wonderful people."

His mother took his face and forced him to look directly at her. "Jesse, we're a family. Yes, what you did was horrible, but our love for you will always be unconditional. You're our son."

Jesse cried so hard he couldn't catch his breath. They just held him.

After a while, Jesse stepped back and said, "I saw Kenny. He's all broken. I did that. Even after all I did, he said he loved me. I don't deserve his love. I'm not worth it."

"Jesse, stop. We'll deal with all of that later. You need to clean up and eat. You need to get some sleep. We'll work on the rest later." His dad pulled him close and kissed his head.

CHAPTER TWO

It took months for Kenny to recover. He almost didn't make it back for the fall semester, but with great determination and his family's help, he made it. It was very quiet on campus; Kenny had to walk with a cane as he was still a little unsteady on his feet. People either avoided him or mobbed him with their caring and support. Much of the football team made sure no one bothered Kenny too much. They helped him get to where he needed to be. It seemed they felt responsible for their teammate's horrible behavior.

The university president called Kenny to his office and asked, "What do you want to happen to the boys that assaulted you?"

"I want them to be left alone. They have to live with what they did to me, and seeing me as I still struggle to make it from one place to another is enough. They have to live with a team that's almost taking better care of me than the hospital staff did, and they have to see that what they did didn't break my spirit, just my heart."

The president sat there stunned for a second. "Wow, you are someone very special, Kenny Van Dever."

Kenny got up and shook his hand. "It's just Ken now." He left.

Jesse wrote:

I saw Kenny in the hospital. What have I done? He wasn't angry or mean, but he won't ever forgive what I did to him. I won't be able to forgive myself, either. I finally told him I loved him, but it doesn't matter anymore now. I just went crazy watching Randy flirt with Kenny, my Kenny. I thought my heart was going to come out of my chest and explode. The more I drank, the more it made me crazy, and when he told me to fuck off, I just lost it. The one person that loved me, just me, now hates me. I don't deserve to live. I see him struggling every day on campus to get around. It hurts my heart so much I can't breathe. My parents and little sister look at me with total disgust, and I'm pretty sure they hate me, too. I have no one left. I need to die.

I'm so sorry, Mom, Dad, and Carrie Ann; you deserve someone so much better than me. I love you so much. Please tell Kenny I will always love him.

Jesse

Jesse finished the note, folded it, and wrote *Mom and Dad* on it. He stood up and moved the chair to where he had fixed the rope. Jesse stepped up onto the chair and placed the rope around his neck. He knocked over the chair and hung himself.

Thankfully, his little sister heard the chair hit the floor and came running in to see what happened. That little ten-year-old girl held him up while screaming hysterically for her mom and dad.

Jesse woke up in the hospital psychiatric ward. His mom and dad were beside themselves, pacing the room. Carrie Ann was holding his hand. "Please, Jesse, don't leave me?"

"I won't," Jesse whispered. His family instantly engulfed him.

His dad tried and tried to speak, but his words wouldn't come out, only sorrow-filled sounds.

Finally, his mom spoke to him quietly and with so much love. "I can't live on this planet without you, my son. I love you with everything inside me and have ever since the moment I first knew you existed. Promise me. You will *never* do this again."

His dad pulled him into a sitting position, sat on the bed, and held him tight. "I love you so much."

Carrie Ann's words hurt him the most. "You did something really stupid and mean and bad, and you did it to someone we love with all our hearts, but you're my big brother, and I need you here." Jesse cried until the tears couldn't fall anymore. His family stayed until visiting hours were over. Exhausted, Jesse fell asleep.

Something startled Jesse awake. He looked around and saw Kenny standing at the door. Since it was late at night, Jesse looked around, confused about whether Kenny was real or not. Plus, the medication made him woozy.

"Jesse, no matter how mad I'm at you, I don't hate you. I still love you with everything my heart has to offer. Live, cuz I can't be without you in this world. Love me enough to live."

Jesse blinked his eyes to make things clearer. When he opened them, Kenny had disappeared.

Jesse told the doctor about Kenny. "I'm sorry, Jesse, but no one could get on this ward without going through security, so it had to be a dream."

Jesse told his dad that he was pretty sure it was real.

Jesse went back to school, but he could see Kenny from nearly every window, out in the courtyard, hobbling around. He was the one who had caused Kenny all that pain. He did love him enough to live, but also enough to know seeing him here on campus hurt Kenny.

He decided to withdraw and moved to a college near his Aunt Kari, three hundred miles away. The arrangements happened quickly. His parents held each other and cried as he pulled out of the driveway, not wanting their son to go, but he told them, "This is the best for everyone, especially for Kenny."

Jesse had nearly killed the one person meant to be his person in the world. The person he wanted to marry and spend the rest of his life with. Now it would never happen. He told his counselor that he needed to learn to live with that.

He kept to himself and worked two part-time jobs so he could pay for his college. His parents helped as much as they could, but Jesse needed to prove he could be a good man and stand on his own.

Jesse got top-notch grades and carried a four-point grade average. He graduated with honors from the pre-med program. He received a full scholarship from Watkins Medical Center at the university.

He and Kenny had always made decisions together. His heart ached with sadness because they could no longer do that. Jesse started to dial Kenny's number several times, but he never could bring himself to follow through.

Jesse made decisions without Kenny and hoped he would be proud of him when he finished.

Jesse talked with his parents weekly. They sometimes told him about Kenny but kept the conversation about him short. Through them, he knew Kenny was working on his doctorate and that he was back to his old self again. Guilt ran through Jesse, the thought that Kenny had to work hard to get back to his old self, and he caused it all.

Jesse found a therapist who helped him with his guilt. He found forgiving himself a lot harder. There were still days when he hated the person he saw in the mirror.

CHAPTER THREE

Medical school was far more intense than the pre-med program. After working in many areas in the medical field, Jesse decided to concentrate on obstetrics and pediatrics. Maybe he could help bring new life into the world.

He threw himself into his studies. His mentor warned him not to burn himself out. Exhaustion caused many medical errors. Jesse never let it happen. He received many accolades for his performance in medical school and ranked at the top of his class. At this rate, he'd graduate *summa cum laude* from medical school.

Three years into medical school, Jesse's mentor arranged for him to do a special study at St. Michael's Children's Hospital in New York City. He worked an internship there for four weeks. He kept extremely busy, and the training proved very taxing. He did find time one evening to hit the night sites of the city.

He wandered around Broadway, taking in the sites. He heard a familiar laugh, looked around, and saw Kenny and Sara. They looked wonderful. Kenny no longer limped nor needed a cane. He looked so handsome and healthy. Just as Jesse tried to duck into the nearest shop so they wouldn't see him, he heard, "Jesse!" Kenny noticed him.

Jesse waited for them to come up to him.

"Jesse, what are you doing in the Big Apple?"

"Hello, Kenny, Sara. I was sent here to do an internship in the neonatal intensive care unit at St. Michaels. I'll be heading back to Watkins at the end of the week. How about you two?"

"Sara's getting married, and she wanted to see if she could find a wedding dress here. And we've seen some shows and enjoyed the sites. It's been a blast."

"Kenny, you look so wonderful."

"No thanks to you," Sara groused.

Kenny took her hand. "Sara, you need to stop." He let go and took Jesse's hand. "Jesse, thank you. You look exhausted, handsome as ever, but exhausted. I'm sorry, but we've got to run. Please take care of yourself."

"You take care, too. It was good seeing you."

Sara and Kenny continued down the sidewalk, and Jesse watched them until they turned the corner. Tears welled up in his eyes. An older lady noticed his sad face and touched his arm. "Are you okay? You look like you just lost your best friend."

"I did, several years ago. I just saw him, and it hurts that we aren't close anymore. Thank you for caring."

"My boy, you're young and still have time to fix whatever happened between you two."

Jesse patted her hand. "You're sweet, but some things are just not fixable."

The lady smiled. "Bullshit, if you want something fixed, you have to do whatever it takes to fix it." She patted his arm and walked away.

Kenny worked hard on his degrees in Psychology. At times, the classwork proved difficult and stressful. His parents fretted and worried he was working too hard. His mother constantly asked him to slow down. Kenny, who now went by Ken, replied, "Mom, I've goals, and I plan on completing them on time."

"You wouldn't have to struggle so much if . . ."

Ken cut her off. "Mother, never again bring up that subject. It's in the past, and I've definitely moved way beyond that. You need to also. Are you hearing me?"

"But—"

"No, Mom, no buts. I'm healthy as a horse, and there's nothing that's stopping me, understood?"

She nodded and then smiled at her son.

The coursework, even though challenging, Ken worked at and excelled. His clinicals proved to be the most challenging part. Ken spent many hundreds of hours working in the hospital psychiatric wards, different clinics, and even at the residential facilities for people with psychological issues. He really loved his work.

Ken graduated with his doctoral degree that spring. He graduated at the top of his class. This gave him many opportunities in his field, but he decided to work with children.

Ken took a job at a children's center. The children had experienced major traumatic events. Some of them stopped speaking and withdrew into their own little worlds.

Ken seemed to work magic with these kids. One day after observing Ken, the psychiatrist who started the center, Dr. Jeffrey Copperton, said, "Dr. Van Dever, you have a unique and wonderful gift. These children blossom under your care. Ken, the boy you just finished working with . . . Andy. He's been here for nearly two years, and no one has been able to reach him. He wouldn't even make eye contact. What do you think brought him out enough to finally look at you? He even speaks to you."

"Dr. Copperton, I'm not a hundred percent sure. I did observe he never looks up. He'll look straight ahead, and he likes to be on his stomach. I read and re-read his history. There was physical, emotional, and sexual abuse at the hands of parents. Andy's safety zone seems to be on his stomach, flat on the floor. So I followed his example. The first few days, he would scoot back from me, but recently, he stopped that and stared at me for long periods. I believe he was trying to figure out if I was friend or foe.

"Two days ago, I rolled a ball to him. He flicked it back with his left hand. That started the first interaction between us. Yesterday, he said the word ball to me, so we played ball. Today he called me *drrr*. Ken. I know he is only five, but I'm pretty sure he can read. He said what he read, dr."

"Ken, you have such an insight for these kids. I'm so glad you came into my practice."

Ken was walking on air. The praise bestowed on him by his boss meant the world to him. As he reached his apartment door, he said out loud, "I hope Jesse will be proud of who I've become."

CHAPTER FOUR

Once again, Christmas came around, and Jesse decided to go home after not attending for nearly eight years. In reality, he decided to go home because his mom begged him. He hated hearing his mother cry. "Mom, I really think it best to stay away."

"Son, it is time to forgive yourself. Come home." He heard the tears in her voice.

Jesse kept another reason for going home a secret. The local hospital in his hometown had offered him the job of head of obstetrics and pediatrics. He planned to look the situation over and decide if he wanted to take the job.

Jesse worried about going home and almost turned around several times, but then decided he needed to see his family.

Jesse stood at the front door for a second before he knocked. When he knocked on the door, excitement exploded when his dad opened that door, and Jesse smiled. His dad quickly pulled him inside. "Janie, our boy is home."

She and his sister came running out of the kitchen. The hugs and kisses that followed felt wonderful.

Jesse felt that everything went pretty well. It felt so good to be home. His sister had grown more beautiful since the last time he saw her. His folks looked older but still acted their happy-go-lucky selves.

Later that day, the doorbell rang. "Jesse, will you get that for me, please? Your dad and sister are out back, and my hands are messy with the stuffing." His mom called out from the kitchen.

"Okay, I got it."

Jesse answered the door, and there stood Kenny, his arm loaded with presents. Jesse thought for sure he'd turn around and leave. But Kenny smiled and stepped into the house. Jesse couldn't believe how beautiful Kenny had become. His golden-brown hair was wavy and curled at the ends. Jesse's stomach flip-flopped when Kenny smiled. Jesse was a little surprised that Kenny wore make-up. It highlighted his beautiful violet eyes.

He liked how Kenny looked. In fact, he looked very sexy, and he told Kenny. "You look so perfect. You're one very handsome man."

"Thanks. Hey, Jesse, how are you? Gosh, I forgot how big you are. I like your curly black hair that length. You're as handsome as ever. And the beard makes you look very distinguished. Your mom told me you had decided on an OB-GYN concentration and are doing extremely well. I'm so proud of you."

"Thanks, Kenny, but you can add pediatrics, too."

Kenny's warm smile made Jesse feel weak-kneed. He reached over to help with the presents, and Kenny flinched.

"Mom, can you come and help Kenny, please."

"Jesse, don't be silly. I'm sorry, but I sometimes react when someone moves quickly toward me." Kenny smiled again at him.

"That's because of me, and I can't tell you how sorry I am. Will you ever be able to forgive me?" he begged.

"Yeah, it was because of you. The keyword is . . . *was*. I've worked through all of that. Yes, I can and have forgiven you a long time ago. Jesse, I love you. That part was easy. I'm just not sure about trusting you yet. We'll see."

Jesse felt a ray of hope for the first time in nearly eight years. "Thank you, Kenny. I love you, too, so much."

Kenny handed Jesse the packages, stood on his tiptoes, and kissed his cheek. "Merry Christmas, Jesse. Oh, yeah, it's Ken. I'm way too old for Kenny." That said, he turned and left through the front door.

Jesse's dad stood behind him, smiling. "You're one lucky son-of-a-bitch. You know that? Not many men get a second chance when they've really fucked up their lives." He hugged his son and walked off. Jesse's broad smile said it all at that moment. Coming home for Christmas — maybe he'd made the right decision after all.

Jesse's family invited Ken's family over to an early Christmas dinner party, just like they'd done for years, and of course, they accepted. When the doorbell rang, Jesse answered it, and there they were with foodstuffs in their arms.

"Don't just stand there gaping. It's cold outside, and the food's getting cold. You've gotten even better looking," Ken's mom, Nanette, said to him. Jesse stepped aside, and they moved past him.

"Merry Christmas." Everyone shouted happily.

Jesse watched as the two families blended together to make one happy, celebrating family. The love flowed around the room. Laughter and the holiday spirit filled the room. He saw the love they all shared and felt for each other. Jesse felt like he wasn't really a part of it. It felt like he stood on the outside, looking in through the window. He stood totally alone. He watched as *his* Kenny laughed and joked with Jesse's sister and Ken's brother. Their parents reminisced about the Christmases celebrated together.

He watched and listened to it all as if he was invisible, watching the families being one large family. Tears flowed from his eyes. Suddenly Ken's arms wrapped around him and pulled Jesse closer to him.

"Jesse, it's time for you to forgive yourself and rejoin the family," Ken said into Jesse's chest.

The sorrows he held in for all these years found their way out, and he sobbed. Nothing could control it. It all just poured out of him. The room went silent. His parents looked grief-stricken, as did Ken's family. Chairs shuffled and scraped the floor. The sound of footsteps came closer. He tensed and tried to get Ken to release him.

"Big guy, you aren't going anywhere without me," Ken said as he tightened his arms around Jesse's waist.

Jesse finally said, "I don't belong here anymore."

He heard the anguished cry from his mother.

Ken's mother said, "You're right. You don't belong here anymore." A collective gasp filled the room. Jesse struggled to get Ken to release him. She continued, "You don't belong here because you refuse to let us love you or accept our forgiveness, and more importantly, because you refuse to forgive yourself. We all love you, Jesse."

"I don't know why any of you would. Kenny, please let me go."

Ken raised his beautiful face, and his violet eyes glistened with tears. "If I let you go, you'll leave, and I've been without you in my life for long enough. I love you, Jesse Hanover, with all my heart. Do you hear me? With all my heart."

"But why?"

"That's simple, Jesse, because I have loved you from the very first day we met, and that never changed, nor will it. You're not the man that hurt me all those years ago. You never were that man. You're the man who wants to bring babies into the world and keep them healthy. You're the man who volunteers at the children's ward to read to the little ones, even though you just finished a three-day work cycle. And even so, you skipped sleeping to read to them nearly every day. That's the real Jesse Hanover, and it's been like that every day since I first met you, always taking care of others."

Ken moved his arms from around his waist and encircled

his neck, "Look at me, big guy. I love you."

"I love you, too, Ken, so damn much it hurts." Tears rolled down Jesse's cheeks, unable to stop them.

Ken pulled his head down to his level, kissing him hard, long, and passionately. It made Jesse breathless. Ken spoke, "Well then, big guy, I guess I'll have to marry you so that no one else can get their hooks into my doctor."

Laughter just exploded out of Jesse. He couldn't remember the last time he truly laughed. "Ken, would you really marry me?" Jesse asked.

The room was tomb silent. It was like the world stood still.

Ken looked over his shoulder and asked, "What are you all waiting for?"

"Your answer!" their families shouted.

"I'm positive that we've already covered this," Ken said, cuddling into Jesse's chest.

Jesse held his breath. Maybe he didn't have the right to ask him.

It was Ken's mother who broke the silence. "Kenneth Van Dever, stop playing games before that poor man crumbles!"

Ken raised his head and looked Jesse in the eyes. "Did you really mean to ask me?"

Jesse nodded.

"Then yes, I will marry you. Not today, but soon. We need time to get to know each other again."

Jesse's knees gave way, and he and Ken crumbled to the floor. Ken hung on as if his life depended on not letting go. "Jesse, are you okay? Do you need a doctor? Jesse, answer me."

Everything he'd wanted to say all these years came tumbling out of his mouth like he had no control. "Ken, I'm so sorry for hurting you back on that terrible day. Alcohol and jealousy overwhelmed me. After that, I saw you in the hospital, all broken and hurt. I wanted to die. You no longer wanted me, and it felt like I had no reason to live."

Ken's voice trembled. "I know. I came to the hospital and begged one of the nurses to let me see you. I had to make sure you were alive. That night, my world started to crumble, too. It was my fault you nearly died."

"Wait, that wasn't a dream like the doctor said it had to be? You really came to me and told me you loved me?" Jesse asked.

Ken nodded quickly.

"And no, Ken, it was not your fault. Every time I saw you limping around that campus, I died a little more inside. I knew as long as I was around, you'd never heal and become the Ken everyone knew and loved. So I transferred. It was a good decision. "

"I've followed your every move, Jesse, and watched over you. Did you know that I'm the psychologist at the local clinic here? After I earned my doctorate in Psychology, I was offered jobs from all over, but I wanted to be close to my family and friends."

"Yeah, I know, your doctoral dissertation was on Trauma and Post Traumatic Stress Disorders in children. I followed your life, too. I'm so proud of your accomplishments."

"Thanks, I'm starving, Jesse. Let's eat."

A collective agreement sounded in the background.

Later that night, Jesse had gone to bed. He felt like a great weight lifted from his heart. He lay on his back and looked at the ceiling. He thought about the events of the day. He smiled when he thought about Ken and the changes that had opened up. Just as he dozed off, he felt the bed dip down. His eyes popped open, and he sat up, startled. He met Ken's loving gaze. Jesse put his hand behind Ken's head and pulled him into a kiss. The kiss turned passionate and needy.

Both men explored and caressed each other's bodies.

Things got very heated. Jesse whispered, "Ken, I've never . . . I mean with anyone, ever."

Ken replied, "Me, either. We'll have to teach each other."

Jesse pulled off his white t-shirt and slipped out of his boxers. He helped Ken with his pajamas. They rolled into each other's arms, kissing and exploring.

Ken reached down and took hold of Jesse's cock. "Holy shit, you're absolutely enormous. Even though you're a mighty big man, this still puts you past the gifted range for sure."

Jesse started laughing at Ken's comments. "Ken, you're quite the stallion yourself. God, I love you."

Their bodies moved in sync with each other. Sounds of passion filled the room. Their climax spilled between them. They stay wrapped in each other's arms. "Jesse?"

"Hmmm?" Jesse replied.

"You're extremely furry, and I mean everywhere," Ken said as his fingers ran down the hair on Jesse's back.

Jesse answered, "I really am. I guess I can work on removing some of it if that's what you would like."

"No, you won't. I love all your fur. I'm like naked. I only have hair on my pits and crotch."

Jesse rolled and pinned Ken down. He brushed his hair off his face and smiled. "I love every inch of you just the way you are. Plus, I think the make-up is sexy, but with or without it, you're one hell of a sexy man."

Jesse gave Ken a quick kiss. "Let's get cleaned up."

"We'll have to be quiet so your family won't be disturbed."

Jesse chuckled. "I think they know. We weren't exactly quiet."

"I'm going to die when I see them."

CHAPTER FIVE

The families spent Christmas Eve at their own homes. Family gifts were traded, and traditions were fulfilled. The Hanovers watch their traditional Christmas movie, *Miracle on 34th Street*.

When the movie started, Jesse's father plopped down next to him. "I heard you had a wonderful time last night. Actually, we all heard you had a wonderful time last night."

Snickers could be heard around the room.

"Oh God, I'm sorry and so embarrassed. I'm so not wanting to have this conversation. Please."

Jesse's little sister responded, "You should have been sneakier."

"Ken surprised me."

Jesse's mom looked startled. "You mean sweet little Ken planned all that?"

Annoyed, Jesse said, "Okay, neither of us have been with someone before. So our exploring got out of hand and became a tiny bit noisy. I'm sorry if we disturbed you."

Carrie Ann freaked out. "I don't want to hear any more about this, or I'll have to stab sharp pencils in my ears. You two are going to have to marry quickly and move in together. Furry? Are you kidding me?"

Jesse put his elbows on his knees and buried his face in his hands. "Dear Lord, make her mute, please God?"

Everyone turned their attention to the movie. Afterward, they started to prepare for the next day's big Christmas dinner.

Ken had thought he would sneak quietly back into the house. *Wrong.* His parents sat at the kitchen table, drinking coffee and chatting. They stopped and looked at Ken as he walked in the door. Both of them smiled at Ken.

His brother walked into the room. "I just heard from Carrie Ann that you and Jesse had quite a . . . how should I put this? Noisy? Is that a good word for it? Yeah, noisy time, that's it." He smirked as he poured a cup of coffee. "Carrie Ann told me she ordered earplugs. I'd say that means you were very noisy. She also said you called Jesse furry."

Ken's parents gaped at him.

He turned several shades of red. "Bob, shut your mouth."

Bob opened his mouth to say something else. Ken lashed out, "One more word, and I'll spill the beans about last Christmas."

Their parents turned and looked at Bob. "Last Christmas? Is there something we need to know about?"

Bob gave them a weird smile. "Nah."

The Ven Devers turned their attention back to Ken. His dad said, "I hope you used protection."

"Paul. He's an adult," his mother scolded and asked, "Is Jesse really furry?"

Ken rubbed his hand over his face as he tried to keep his composure. "I'm not going to have this discussion."

"It's okay, dear. I'll just ask him when he gets here." His mother folded her hands on the table and smiled.

"I'll duct tape your mouth if you do."

Ken's parents and brother burst into laughter. Ken did the walk of shame all the way to his room. He immediately called Jesse, and he answered right away. "Your sister has a big mouth."

"Yeah, I know."

"My parents know everything. I'll never be able to live this down."

"It will pass," Jesse confidently said.

"Jesse, they know about furry."

"I'm going to choke her. Can we spend tonight together? But this time in your room?"

"No, we're not spending the night at my or your parent's house."

"Ken, did I do something wrong? You don't want to spend the night together?"

"Jesse, I don't live with my parents. I just spent a few nights here because driving back and forth is a pain. I have my own place. We'll go there after dinner tonight. Okay? Jesse? Are you there?"

"I'm here. I just thought for a minute you didn't want to be with me."

"What! Why would you think that? I'm never letting you go. I'll see you later. I have to go and watch the family movie. I think I know all the lines in *The Christmas Carol* by heart. Mom's cooking up a storm, so I better help her." They watched the movie, ate supper, and opened gifts.

Ken met Jesse in the driveway right after dinner. Jesse asked, "Did your parents give you a hard time about going over to your place?"

"They started to until I told them I was hosting tonight. Dad said all dad-like, *Well, then, I think you made the right choice. Be back by nine tomorrow morning.* I promised we would."

Ken's apartment was pretty large and beautifully decorated. Jesse got the whirlwind tour.

Ken took Jesse's hand and let him into his bedroom. "What do you think about this?"

Jesse looked around and said, "*Oooo-wee*, this is fancy. That king-size bed was a good idea."

"Jesse, we can talk about the furnishing or — "

Jesse picked Ken up and gently lifted him onto the bed. "Honey, I just can't get enough of you," Jesse said as he started undressing his lover. "You're so beautiful."

After just one passionate kiss, Ken fired up and started to quickly take off Jesse's clothes. "Jesse, I need you. I want you to make love to me so desperately."

"Baby, just let me finish undressing, and I'm all yours." They explored one another's bodies and learned about love-making from each other.

Ken and Nanette banned Bob and Paul from the kitchen as they got in the way. Besides, Ken and his mother had the entire cooking thing down-pat. They chatted as they prepared the dishes.

"Ken, how long are you going to make Jesse wait?"

"For what, Mom?"

"For you two to be together and married."

"I was thinking maybe two or three ... days. We were thinking about getting married soon."

"I thought you were going to say years. You're a little shit. You know that? I nearly popped you with this rolling pin. Have you two really thought this thing out?"

"Mom, I've missed so much. I don't want to be without him anymore. He's my soulmate, my life, and his touch sets me on fire."

"I get that, honey. That's how I feel about your father. I know the Hanovers are the same. Do you think Carrie Ann and Bob feel like that, too?"

Ken coughed in surprise. "How long have you known about them?"

"From the very first kiss. They've mooned over each other for years. I'll tell you a little secret. I think they've been playing it cool, waiting for you and Jesse to get your lives straightened out. Oh, Ken, your eyeliner is crooked, and you have two different colored eyeshadows on. Hectic morning? Hmmm?"

"Are you kidding me?"

"Nope, not kidding."

Ken took off for the bathroom. He was gone about twenty minutes and returned. "How's that?"

"So much better. You look perfect."

"Thank goodness no one saw me."

"Oh, honey, Bob took pictures. Everyone's going to see."

Ken was very angry until he noticed something on the table. "Mom, look what's on the table. Bob's phone."

Ken picked it up and scrolled through it, found his pictures, and deleted them. He scrolled a little farther and froze. He started making gagging sounds.

His mother panicked. "Ken, what's wrong? Are you okay?"

"Mom, I just saw nudes of my brother. I may go blind. Not only that, but there are some of Carrie Ann, too."

"Shut the front door! There better not be. I will break his—"

"Dick?"

"Hush." His mother snapped at him.

"He's a grown man. There's nothing you can do."

"Wanna bet? By the way, call Jesse and see if he and his dad can come over and help set things up."

"I did that already. They'll be over around two this afternoon."

Ken texted Jesse.

Ken—*I wish your furry body was next to mine. Love you.*

Jesse—*Ah, I'm working with Mom right now, and I don't need to get all worked up. Love you, too.*

Ken—*I miss you, stud man.*

Jess—*Keep it up, and I'll come over and take you in your mom's kitchen.*

Ken—*Sorry, see you soon. XOXOXOX.*

The Hanovers gathered their foodstuffs for the Christmas dinner and walked next door. Ken met them at the door. He helped carry everything into the kitchen. The family did their Christmas chatter. Jesse pulled Ken under the mistletoe and kissed him.

Bob snidely remarked, "What, you two didn't get enough last night? I could barf."

Ken smiled. "I know just how you feel. I had to take deep breaths after the picture I saw this morning. So I wouldn't throw up."

"What pictures?" Jesse asked.

Bob suddenly said, "I forgot about the pictures. I took several of Ken that you have to see." He took out his phone and stood next to Jesse so he could see. But Jesse only saw naked pictures, first of Bob and then Carrie Ann.

Bob realized something was up. "What the hell, where are the pictures I took of you this morning?" He looked at Jesse and saw that he was pissed. "Wait, you didn't see the pics of me and—"

"I fucking did. Do you want me to kill you now or kill you after supper?"

Ken rescued his brother. "Jesse, your sister is an adult, as is my brother. They can't help it if they are in love and going a little wild. Even though I think sending nudies to each other is incredibly stupid, it's not for us to judge."

Carrie Ann walked into the room. "Hey, you handsome men, what's up? You all look so serious."

Jesse snarled and said, "Nothing much, just nude pictures of you and your idiot boyfriend."

"Oh. My. God. Do Mom and Dad know about this?" Carrie Ann asked as she turned very pale.

Ken laughed and said, "Well, probably by now. Seeing as my mom knows."

A voice roared from the kitchen. "Carrie Ann Hanover and Robert Paul Van Dever, where are you?" It was Barry Hanover. Both sets of parents entered the room. None looked happy.

Ken cheerfully said to Jesse, "Have you seen how much snow we're getting? Let's check it out. Okay?"

"Are you kidding, Ken? I want to hear this," Jesse told him.

Both sets of parents said, "No, you don't."

Paul added, "Take coats. You may be out there for a while."

Jesse and Ken walked around in the snow, holding hands and occasionally kissing. Out of nowhere, a snowball suddenly hit Jesse in the face. "What the fuck?" Jesse looked around and saw Sara.

"Jesse, why are you polluting the area? Aren't you banned from here, like forever?" It was then she saw Ken. Her eyes nearly bugged out of her head when she saw that Jesse held Ken's hand.

Her husband took one look at her and stopped her in her tracks. "Sara, this isn't your business. What they do together is never going to be your concern. You're not his mother, sister, or wife. Understand?"

"I saved his life. I get to have a say in this." Sara marched over to Jesse and Ken. She got up in Jesse's face and started screaming at him. "You don't belong here. Let go of his hand right now. Go climb back under the rock you came from, you piece of shit."

Ken stepped between Sara and Jesse and pushed her back. "Have you lost your damn mind? You have absolutely no say in who I date, fall in love with, or marry. If you ever pull this shit again, I'll never speak to you ever again. Apologize right now." Ken was over the top angry.

"I will not."

"Then go home. What happened all those years ago is over. Jesse and I are in a permanent relationship. Either be on board or go home."

Sara stood gaping at Ken. She took another step back, and then fury showed all over her face. "I saved your life, and you choose him over me?"

"Sara, I'm not doing that. You are. I don't have to choose one or the other. I can love you both."

Vlad stepped next to his wife and put his arm around her waist. He spoke to her calmly and lovingly, "Sara, what if Ken had acted like you're acting? What if he made you choose me or him? Wouldn't that have torn you apart?"

"You didn't nearly beat me to death." Sara started crying.

Ken took both of her hands. "Neither did *this* Jesse. He suffered enough and still is having a hard time forgiving himself. He's made such good progress, and I don't want him to backslide. So I won't allow anyone to say or do things that could make him doubt himself. I love you, but I love him, too."

"Sorry," Sara said. She glared at Jesse and stormed off into Ken's parents' home. Vlad followed quickly.

Ken turned to Jesse, and he saw tears rolling down his cheeks.

"No, you don't. You don't get to let her words confuse what we've become. You're my fiancé and the love of my life. She's just angry, but she'll come around. Like you, she's a very good person."

Jesse quickly wiped away the tears with his coat sleeve. He got down on one knee and said, "Kenny, I have loved you all of my life, and I never believed I would be part of your life again." Reaching into his pocket, he pulled out something. "Will you marry me?" He opened his hand. There was a beautiful gold ring with diamonds embedded all around it.

Ken said, "I thought we covered this just the other day."

Ken then noticed the ring in the palm of Jesse's hand. "You're not fooling, are you?" Ken's eyes swelled with tears as he took the ring and put it on his left ring finger. "Yes, I'll marry you, Jesse. I guess this makes me officially engaged to you. Stand up so I can thank you properly."

Jesse stood, and Ken threw himself at Jesse, causing him to fall backward into the snow. "Ooof," Jesse grunted. "Ken, you got me in the nuts."

Ken rolled off him and said, "Are you going to be all right? I'm so sorry."

Jesse rolled back and forth, holding his crotch. It took a few minutes for Jesse to recover. "Ken, we'll need these guys, so try not to do that again."

"Jesse, I'm so terribly sorry. Should I kiss them and make it better?"

Jesse paused as he thought about it. "No."

"When did you have time to get this beautiful ring?" Ken asked as he helped Jesse up.

"Remember when I ran into you in New York City?"

"Yes."

"Well, after you and Sara left, I had a bit of a meltdown. This sweet older lady touched my arm and said that I looked like I'd just lost my best friend. I told her I did, and it was all my fault. She smiled at me and told me that I still had time to fix things. While walking back to the hospital, I was praying she was right. I walked past this little jewelry store, and there was your ring. I hoped it was a sign, and it was."

"Jesse, you've had it all this time, waiting for me? I'm going to start bawling. God, I love you. Marry me right after Christmas, okay?"

"How about New Year's Eve? If we can work it out," Jesse suggested.

"Perfect."

CHAPTER SIX

K en and Jesse returned to Jesse's home only to find people sitting in the living room scowling at each other. Jesse asked, "What's going on?"

Bob filled them in. "Sara is being a butt. Vlad is mad at Sara. Carrie Ann and I are getting married. Mom and Dad are hoping it's a girl. Paul and Nanette are hoping for a boy. Yes, we're pregnant. Carrie Ann is mad at her parents. I'm mad at you two just because I can be. That just about sums things up."

Ken looked surprised. "You're what? Pregnant? How does that happen in this day and age?" Ken took a quick glance at Jesse. He immediately saw that Jesse looked very angry, so he stepped between Bob and Jesse and said, "Bob, run."

Bob took one look at Jesse and took off out the back door.

Ken held Jesse back. "Honey, it's Christmas. I know you're upset, but Bob and Carrie Ann are adults. Take a deep breath and calm down. I love you." Ken cleared his throat to get everyone's attention. "FYI, everyone, Jesse and I are officially engaged." Ken showed off his ring. "We also want to be married on New Year's Eve if we can work out all the details."

The families froze and stared at Ken and Jesse. Finally, Carrie Ann jumped out of her seat, hurried over, and hugged them both. "I'm so happy for you both."

Ken held her tight. "We're so happy for you two. Go get Bob before he freezes to death."

The rest of the family joined in the celebration. Everyone congratulated them, everyone except Sara. She just stared,

red-faced and sneering. Finally, she marched up to Ken, pulled her arm back, and swung to slap him. Jesse caught her by the wrist and held it tight.

"Sara, don't ever do that again. It would break Ken's heart." He released her wrist.

The room fell silent. Ken gaped in disbelief at Sara. They stared at each other. Vlad put his hands on Sara's shoulders and said, "Striking out in anger is not a good thing, right?" Sara slowly turned to face him. The realization of what she'd almost done hit her hard, and she leaned into Vlad and cried.

Ken walked up and rubbed her shoulders. "It's all right. We all make mistakes, and those who love us will always forgive them."

She quickly turned and hugged him. "I'm so terribly sorry."

Jesse had joined Ken. He stood directly behind him. Ken said, "I'm starving, let's eat."

The entire group suddenly started scurrying around. They brought out the food, and everyone sat at the table. Barry Hanover bowed his head and said, "Lord, thank you for the people at this table. It feels good not having an empty seat. Thank you for this wonderful food prepared by all. Amen."

They passed bowls and filled plates. At first, everyone ate silently. But then Bob noticed the ring on Ken's finger. "So, are you two officially engaged?"

Ken's face lit up. He showed everyone the ring Jesse gave him. "Yes, we are. Have you thawed out yet? I wouldn't get caught alone with Jesse for a while. He's a doctor, after all, and knows about reproduction and how to prevent it."

The table exploded with laughter. Everyone enjoyed the joke except Sara. She sat there scowling and glaring at Jesse.

Ken started to speak to her, but Jesse stopped him. "Ken, leave it alone."

People continued to eat and chat amongst themselves. Sara still glared.

Ken picked up his spoon, scooped up some mashed potatoes, and flicked them right on Sara's face. She stood up indignantly and threw her napkin on the table.

Ken smirked and said, "Isn't that what you did to me when I was being a jerk about you and Vlad? Hmmm?"

Sara fish-mouthed, sputtered, and then wiped the potatoes off her face. She sat back down, and after a moment of silence, Jesse snorted a suppressed laugh. Then Ken laughed. Vlad started laughing, and finally, unable to stop herself, Sara laughed.

Sara pointed her fork at Jesse. "You hurt him, I'll make you suffer."

Jesse nodded slowly. "Fair enough."

Bob suddenly leaned forward to look at Ken and Jesse. "Carrie Ann told me that you two are looking to get hitched on New Year's Eve. Sorry, buds, that ain't going to happen. There's a ten-day waiting period after you apply for your license. So the soonest would be around the tenth."

"And how do you know that information?" Sara asked, ever so coyly.

All heads turned and looked at Bob. "Oh shit, Carrie Ann, help."

"Man up, for God's sake. We got the information when we applied for our marriage license."

The families chatted and told stories for the rest of the meal. Everyone looked to be enjoying the dinner. Ken placed his hand on Jesse's leg and tried to slide it up to cop a feel.

Jesse leaned over and whispered in Ken's ear, "You need to stop and remove your hand before the big guy gets excited. I need to get up and go to the restroom. You're moving your hand in the wrong direction. Please, Ken."

There was a sudden thud under the table. Ken yelped,

"Ow. Sara, that hurt."

"Get a room, you perv. There! I rescued you, Jesse."

Jesse smiled, winked, and got up. He briefly left the room. When he returned, he kissed Ken's ear and sat down. "Sara, Ken told me you're an RN at the hospital. Does it have a good work environment?"

"It's great, why?" Sara looked slightly confused.

"I've been offered the opportunity to head the OBGYN and Pediatric centers there. I haven't accepted the position yet, as I still need to meet with the Chief of Staff and the board of directors. I want to work in a hospital with a friendly, caring staff and loving environment." Ken looked at Jesse with a very shocked expression. "Honey, I was going to tell you tonight. Please don't be upset with me. I've, or rather we've had a lot going on. So please tell me you're okay with this."

The entire room became silent, and all eyes focused on Jesse. "Okay, so you all know. I've been offered a job heading up several departments at Riverside Hospital. I haven't told anyone for several reasons. First, I still haven't accepted the position because I need to review the job and working conditions. Also, so much has happened with Ken that it hasn't been a priority until now."

Sara's expression turned smug. "Good thing I'm on the placement and hiring committee. I'll have to really scrutinize your resume and credentials."

Jesse smiled and said pleasantly, "Sara, I'm not interviewing for a position. I'm deciding whether to take the offer that the board and Chief of Staff offered me."

Sara's smugness disappeared. "I see, so they just skipped the committee?"

Ken interrupted. "Sara, Jesse's a very much sought-after physician. He finished top in his medical fields. We'd be lucky to have him on the staff of our hospital. I happen to know he was offered several positions all over the country. I've been keeping an eye on him."

"Have you been stalking me?" Jesse teased.

Jesse's mom, Janie, stood up like she was going to speak. Her mouth moved, but nothing came out.

Jesse pushed back his chair and quickly moved to his mother. "Mom, are you okay?"

Finally able to speak, Janie asked, "So you are coming home and staying?"

"Mom, I said that I was looking at the position. I haven't made a decision yet. I have a meeting with Dr. Rogers and the board on Tuesday." He tilted her head up so their eyes met. "I haven't made a decision and can't until I meet with them."

Janie's eyes pooled with tears. "I can hope, can't I?"

Ken left the table and disappeared into the next room. Jesse saw the anguish on his face and went after him. Ken stood looking out the window in the kitchen.

Jesse approached Ken. He put his arms around his shoulders and rested his chin on top of Ken's head. "I know we need to talk. I promise, I never intended to have everything come out like this."

"I know." Ken turned in Jesse's arms and faced him. "What if you don't take this offer? What happens to us?"

"What do you mean? What's going to happen to us? We're still us. I want to marry you and love you forever."

"Jesse, if you take a job somewhere else, do you expect me just to give up the job I love and follow you?"

"Oh, Kenny, of course not. I expect I'll be doing a lot of traveling. But let's not get ahead of ourselves. I have to meet with Dr. Rogers and the board. If the job is just what I want, I'll take it. If not, we'll work from there." Jesse pulled Ken in tight. "I want a job that allows me to do the things I was trained to do and love. Mostly, I want to love you with everything I have inside of me."

Ken stepped back. "Jesse, look me in the eyes. No more se-crets. I want to know first, not with the group. I want us to make decisions together. Jesse, I know you worked very hard to get where you are now. But so have I. I, too, want to have a job that I love but, more importantly, where I can help chil-dren. Can I go with you on Tuesday?"

"Of course, I was about to ask you to do just that. Ken, I want you by my side always."

Ken pulled Jesse's face down and kissed him. "There may be one downside to the job here."

"Really, what would that be?"

Ken smiled. "You'd be working with Sara."

Laughing, Jesse said, "Yeah, but I will outrank her. We'd better get back in there so I can calm the shitstorm I stirred up."

Ken wrapped his arm around Jesse's waist, and they re-turned to the dining table. Ken sat down. He noticed that all eyes were on him and Jesse. "We're okay. Jesse and I are on the same page. So, you all will find out what's going on after we meet with the administration at the hospital on Tuesday. Now, on to another subject. Carrie Ann and Bob, what are your plans? Do you need our help with anything? Like ar-rangements or finances? We're here for you. I promise."

Bob and Carrie Ann beamed with gratitude. The conversa-tion moved to them and what they were planning.

Ken noticed Sara and Vlad whispering, and Sara shook her head, not agreeing with whatever Vlad said.

"Okay, you two, something is up. Spill."

Vlad nudged her. "Honey, it's okay. Tell him."

Ken quickly tapped his glass with his spoon. The ringing got everyone's attention. "Sara and Vlad have an announcement. Okay, Sara, you have everyone's attention. What is it?"

Sara squinted at Ken and said in a fake, mean voice, "I really hate you."

She then stood and pulled Vlad up next to her. "We're having a baby." Joyful sounds filled the room. Then came hugs and kisses. Eventually, the couple sat down.

"I can't believe you kept that secret from me," Ken playfully scolded.

Sara leaned forward. "For five months. And as for keeping secrets . . ." Her finger flipped back and forth between Ken and Jesse.

Ken blushed. He got up, hurried around the table, and hugged her.

When they returned to Ken's apartment, he told Jesse, "This Christmas was absolutely the most perfect one I've ever had."

"Ken, I'm so afraid that this is all a dream, and I'll wake up and be back in the nightmare of life without you."

Ken pinched his butt hard. "See, it's real."

Jesse had him scooped up and carried him into the bedroom within seconds.

CHAPTER SEVEN

Tuesday came, and Jesse woke Ken with some very passionate lovemaking. After showering and breakfast, they went to dress for the meeting. "Jesse, should I leave off the make-up?"

"Why would you?"

"I don't want to do anything to jeopardize you getting the job."

"Honey, it's not about me getting the job. It's whether I take the job. It's already mine if I want it, and I have that in writing."

Jesse held Ken's hand as they entered the hospital. The receptionist directed them to the administration offices. The administrative secretary showed them to a conference room. Jesse opened the door and let Ken enter first. Jesse collided with Ken because he abruptly stopped. At a large table sat the board of directors, the Chief of Staff, and — big surprise — Sara.

Jesse stepped forward and asked, "What is going on here?"

The Chief of Staff, Dr. Harlon Rogers cleared his throat. "Good morning, Dr. Hanover. We have some concerns after receiving information from the Director of Nursing, Mrs. Sara Sarcoff. Also, I was unaware you were bringing someone with you."

Ken visibly bristled. "Knock it off, Harlon. You know exactly who I am, and knowing that loudmouth woman sitting over there, you know that I'm Dr. Hanover's fiancé."

Dr. Roger's surprised expression and the look he gave Sara absolutely indicated he did not know. "I'm sorry, I wasn't informed of that."

Ken continued. "We have a pretty good idea of where this is going and would gladly discuss the matter with you." Ken looked toward Sara, and his voice became harsh and louder, "But first, I want that woman out of here right now."

"Sara, you are dismissed," Dr. Rogers said.

The authority in his voice clearly caught Sara off guard. She sat for a moment and then got up and left. She stopped and opened her mouth when she got to Ken and Jesse.

Jesse stepped forward and blocked her from approaching Ken. "Just leave."

Jesse stepped forward and sat down. Ken came up from behind him and placed his hands on his shoulders. "I'm going to leave and let Jesse explain about this, and then I'll come back in and clarify any lingering questions. I have some quick business to attend to."

Ken left the room, and as he stepped outside, he saw Sara standing there.

"I did this for you." Sara sounded very pompous.

Ken walked up and stood in front of her. "No, you didn't do this for me. You did this because you're a spiteful bitch. You hate the idea of Jesse and I being together. FYI, Jesse had already told them about what happened ten-plus years ago. But you had to show your ass and blow it all up again. I bet it was an Academy-winning performance. Well, Sara, you only accomplished one thing. You have cut me, my family, Jesse, and his family from your life. Never contact any of us again. I hope this got you what you were after." Ken turned and went back to the conference room.

Sara started crying. "Ken, I love you. I have to protect you."

"No, Sara, you don't. You love the idea of being my savior, not me, or else you wouldn't have deliberately hurt me like this."

Ken went back inside the room. He found the room atmosphere had become lighter.

"Dr. Van Dever, we'd like to ask you a few questions if you're okay with that."

Ken shrugged. "Sure, why not? And we all know each other. It's Ken."

Dr. Rogers smiled and started. "Ken, why didn't you press charges against Jesse?"

"Because I knew it wasn't who he was. If it had been just him and I, that incident would have never happened. He was only twenty-two, just realizing that his feelings for me were way beyond friendship. He'd been drinking, egged on by the people he was with, and it didn't help that I was flirting with someone else. He got rude. I got mad and left.

"I found out later that Jesse told his team he needed to talk with me. They machoed up and started goading him. They came to me several months later and told me what they'd done. After that, Jesse's guilt overrode everything else, and he tried to take his life. I thought my heart would stop beating. I forgave Jesse and everyone else that was involved a long time ago. That was not *my* Jesse. My Jesse was and is loving, kind, gentle, and cares about helping others. We have healed and moved on. He asked me to marry him, and I said yes."

"Can I ask you one more thing?"

Ken nodded.

"Why did Sara come and present her bizarre rendition of this event?"

"Sara did help me, probably saved my life. But she feels she's earned the right to run my life and control every aspect of it. Five years ago, we had a major falling out, and she stepped back. She then had time to fall in love and marry. It started up again when she found out Jesse and I were together. I have cut ties with her."

"We have all the information we need. Thank you, Ken. Jesse, Dr. Hanover, our offer still stands. I hope you understand that we had to look into his matter."

Jesse smiled and took Ken's hand. "I understand why you had to check everything out. Why don't we take a tour of the facilities and talk about the position?"

The group walked and talked as they toured. Dr. Rogers introduced Jesse to many of the staff. Two hours later, they returned to the conference room.

"So, Dr. Hanover, what do you think of our hospital and of our offer?" Dr. Roger asked.

Jesse smiled and took Ken's hand. "Well, gentlemen, I've decided to take the position you've offered me."

The entire group stood, shook Jesse's hand, and welcomed him to the fold. When Dr. Rogers shook his hand, he said, "Jesse, you're one lucky SOB. Your Ken is someone very special."

"You're right, and he's all mine." Jesse glanced at Ken and winked. They left and walked down the hall to the reception area. There sat Sara. She stood up and looked at Ken and Jesse with a pleading look. Jesse moved Ken to his other side, putting himself between Ken and Sara.

"Ken, Kenny. Please," Sara begged.

Ken stopped and looked stone-faced at Sara. "No, just no. We are nothing now. You're a vindictive bitch."

Jesse blocked Sara from seeing Ken. "Sara, I'm not sure why you did this. I don't keep what I did back then a secret. They knew all about it. Plus, most of them remembered the whole incident as they all lived here back then. But you had to go there and not just tell them what you knew. You had to go into a dramatic presentation and add lies to the whole scenario. Why? Why would you do that? I know you hate me, and hurting me was your big goal, but instead, you hurt Ken. You hurt him and broke his heart. Are you happy now? Are you proud of the pain you caused him?"

Sara sobbed. "I was just trying to protect the hospital from scandal down the road. More importantly, I was only protecting my friend from you hurting him again."

Ken started to fall apart. He stepped around Jesse and walked up to Sara. "No, that's not why. You were losing control and couldn't stand it. That's the only reason you did this. Have a great life, and get some help. Goodbye." He turned and buried his face into Jesse's chest.

"Come on, sweetheart. I'll take you home." Jesse and Ken started walking away, but Jesse stopped and said to Sara without looking at her, "Sara, I hope everything works out for you and your family."

They left, leaving Sara crying.

Jesse took Ken to the Van Dever home. Ken fell apart when he walked into the house. At first, his parents attacked Jesse, but he stood up for himself.

"This is not on me. Sara caused Ken's current emotional state." Jesse explained the situation and what had gone down, how Sara tried very hard to sabotage his job. They were not only upset but became angry with the whole ordeal.

Ken's parents asked, "What about the job?"

Jesse hugged Ken. "They offered, and I decided to take up their offer."

Ken reached up and stroked Jesse's cheek. "He did that for me. I know he could have taken a more prestigious, higher-paying job, but he didn't. He did that all because he loves me."

Jesse smiled. "That's partly true. But not entirely. I took the position because it's a good one, and I'm needed here."

The two of them discussed the situation with his parents.

While the discussion was going on, Bob came rushing in. "Jesse, Ken, are you okay? I heard about the shitshow Sara pulled. There's talk of her losing her job."

Jesse's eyes widened with surprise. "Ken, is that what you want, for her to be totally disgraced? That would make us not any better than she is. You told me she was a terrific nurse and loved helping people. I don't feel right about crushing her."

Ken took Jesse's face in his hands. "This is why I love you so much. Your heart is so big, and you wear it on your sleeve. Let's both stop that before it goes overboard."

The two of them split up and started calling people. Jesse called the board of directors. He spoke to each one and convinced them not to take action against Sara.

Ken called and convinced Dr. Rogers to only reprimand her.

They rejoined the family and explained what was happening.

Bob said, "You two are too damn big-hearted. I would have hung her out to dry."

Jesse smirked. "Well, there was one caveat. I'm going to be her boss. They put me over the Director of Nursing at my request."

Everyone sat in stunned silence until Ken started to laugh. "She's going to shit herself."

Ken's parents and brother joined in laughing.

Jesse just shook his head. "I just may have started a new shitstorm. Ken, we need to tell my parents about our decision. Mom will stroke out with happiness when she finds out I'm taking the position."

Jesse's and Ken's families decided there would be no contact with Sara until she made amends for her attack on Jesse. Jesse didn't like that idea much. He reminded them she was pregnant and that they were her only family.

Jesse and Ken went to the courthouse the next day to get their marriage license. Bob was wrong. They didn't need to wait ten days, because the registrar was there and signed it right away. She told them, "I'm issuing this right away because I don't want our new doctor getting cold feet and disappearing."

"How on earth did you know about me accepting the opening here?" Jesse asked.

"Oh, honey, it's all over town. So is the incident with Sara Sarcoff. I've known her since she was a toddler. I don't know what happened to her."

"She's hormonal due to her pregnancy, so she got emotional and thus got carried away. We still love her dearly. She's Ken's best friend," Jesse gently answered.

The registrar looked a bit embarrassed.

Jesse saw the look of surprise on Ken's face. They gathered their license, thanked everyone, and left. Ken took Jesse's arm and hugged it. He smiled and said, "This is why I love you so damn much."

Jesse smiled so broadly. "Ken, I know you're angry and have every right to be, but I think we need to fix this with Sara."

Ken looked up and met Jesse's loving eyes. "We will, but not just yet. She needs to really understand that I'm not her possession, and I don't owe her my life, just my gratitude. She'll come over tomorrow because Vlad will make her. She'll have had some time to think things over until then."

Jesse stopped and glanced over to Ken. "How do you know Vlad will make her come over tomorrow?"

"Because you have this ginormous heart, and you called him and asked him."

"How on earth? I called him while in the car, and you were in the house. How did you know?" Jesse gave Ken a suspicious look.

"Jesse, you can't stand to see anyone suffer. That big heart of yours won't allow it, even if you must bury your feelings. Jesse, I want to tell you something you may not know or remember." Ken's eyes welled with tears. They got into the car.

"Ken, you're scaring the shit out of me."

Ken took Jesse's hand and squeezed it tight. "The night I got hurt."

Jesse started to speak.

"Shhh, let me say this. That night you grabbed me? I saw the fury in your eyes. It was like you were someone else. Then you hit me, and I went down. Jesse, in that instant, your whole demeanor changed. I saw the horror in your face at what you'd done. You stood there like you couldn't see or hear what was happening. All the other guys involved that night came to me and begged me to forgive them. Each one said the same thing. You only slapped me, and then you freaked out. You stood there frozen."

Jesse tried not to lose it, but the noise kept escaping. He covered his face and cried. He finally calmed and said, "Kenny, I'm so fucking sorry. I only remember I slapped you, and you fell. I have tried and tried to—" Jesse couldn't catch his breath.

"Jesse, stop, please. I didn't tell you this to make you sad. I just thought you should know the whole truth. You're not the horrible villain you believe you are. To be honest, I thought you already knew this."

"Kenny, even so, if I hadn't hit you, they wouldn't have joined in. It's still all my fault. Do you still want to marry me? I won't blame you if you want out."

Ken raised his voice in anger. "Jesse, are you stupid or what? You're my person, the one who was meant to make me whole. A life without you won't be a life. I love everything about you." Ken's voice softened. "Mr. Furry, take me home. I plan on wrapping myself in fur tonight."

Jesse chuckled, and then his sexy voice deepened. "Ken, you're the only person I have ever loved or ever will love. You're my entire world. I love you and always will. Mr. Furry? Huh? Well, Mr. Furry wants to do more than just wrap fur around you."

CHAPTER EIGHT

The two families sat around the dining table at Jesse's folk's house. They were planning Ken and Jesse's wedding. Ken and his mother were arguing. "Mom, this is going to be a small wedding. I mean small."

"But, honey, we must invite your grandparents, aunts, and uncles, cousins, and some close friends."

"No, Mom, we don't. You can invite twenty-five people, and you choose who you want."

Janie, Jesse's mom, interrupted, "Twenty-five? Are you kidding? My bare minimum is sixty people."

Ken threw his hands in the air, shaking them around like he had a seizure or something. "Sixty? Are you all crazy?"

Janie stared at him and said, "That's the very bare minimum. My good list is one hundred and eight."

Ken's mom said, "My good list is one hundred four."
Both mothers put on a face that Ken called the *You'll never win this battle* look.

Jesse leaned in and whispered very softly, "I love it when you get all assertive, it really makes me horny. Let the top number be two hundred twenty-five. You'll never win, so surrender now, or I'll have to toss you on the table and make love to you here and now."

Ken's gaze locked with Jesse's. A slightly shocked expression popped up. "Oh, okay, fine, I give up. If I don't, Jesse will ravish me right here on the table."

Ken's dad spit out his coffee and choked a little. Jesse turned beet red and ran his hand over his face.

Ken realized what had just fallen out of his mouth and quickly said, "Two hundred and twenty-five, and that's the absolute maximum period, no exceptions. Oh, yeah, twenty-five of those are for Jesse and me. How in the hell Jesse and I will afford this is beyond me. Now, you two women go harass Bob and Carrie Ann."

Nanette nearly shouted, "Wait, how many groomsmen are you two having?"

Ken opened his mouth, but Jesse beat him to the punch. "Carrie Ann will stand with me and Bob with Ken. That's it. Plus, Sara will be the stage manager for this production." Jesse made it clear that was it.

"So, you've forgiven Sara?" Janie asked.

Ken said, "Sorta, but she doesn't know it yet, so keep it to yourselves. She and Vlad are coming over to my apartment later today."

Nanette told them, "Sweethearts, don't worry about the cost. We're paying for the whole thing. Just like we'll pay for Carrie Ann's and Bob's wedding. Hush, no arguing."

Ken and Jesse tried to protest, but it was in vain.

Several hours later, Sara and Vlad arrived at Ken and Jesse's apartment. Jesse met them at the door and invited them in. They sat down. Ken brought in some light refreshments and then sat next to Jesse. Sara cleared her throat. "Just want to say how sorry I am. I acted like a complete asshole. Please forgive me."

Jesse spoke before Ken could. "Sara, thanks for that, but we aren't going to discuss that right now. I'm still pissed about it, so for now, let it go. We didn't ask you to come here to apologize. We asked you here to be our stage manager, director, coordinator, or whatever you want to call it for our wedding. You're bossy and mean enough to handle our mothers, and we want you to be part of the whole thing. Ken loves you so much, and I don't want him to be sad anymore. So, are you interested?"

Sara looked at Ken and then back to Jesse. She sat, barely moving. Her eyes filled with tears, and then they rolled down her cheeks. Her husband put his arm around her and pulled her close while she cried. After a few minutes, she gathered herself and sat up straight. "Are you both sure? I would love to do this, but only if you both want this."

Jesse answered, "Sara, Ken and I love you, but we're still pissed about what went down. This get-together is my doing. I did it out of love for you two. I can't take seeing people hurting. I'm totally on board with your involvement in our wedding. I can't imagine not having you there. So, are you going to be our sergeant-major?"

Sara jumped up and hugged Ken and Jesse. "Of course I will. Do you have a venue? Flowers? Guest list? Caterer? Or anything yet?"

Both men shook their heads no.

"You're kidding. Tell me you're kidding." Sara sounded very concerned.

Jesse smiled. "Not kidding. Oh, one more thing. The wedding is next Saturday, so you have seven whole days to help us get ready."

Sara, wide-eyed, said, "Now, you really are kidding, right?"

Jesse chuckled. "Not kidding. I start work in just over two weeks. So we need the wedding on that day. Plus, I want to go on a honeymoon with Ken for a week. So, there you have it."

"*Oookay*, so how many guests will there be, or could there be?" Sara hesitantly asked.

Ken said, "I have limited our mothers to two hundred twenty-five. I wanted only a total of one hundred, but Jesse seduced me into the larger number. Our mothers will help you, I promise."

"Okay, I'm on this. Jesse, call the moms and tell them I'm coming over right away. Vlad, I need the car. You, Ken, and Jesse go get something to eat and go bowling or something. I'll meet you all at Ken's mother's house in four hours. Go."

Ken, Jesse, and Vlad arrived four hours later at Ken's mom's house. They opened the door only to be met by Ken and Jesse's fathers. "Don't come in here. Turn around and run," Paul said to them.

Barry added, "It's a trap."

Just as Ken and Jesse tried to turn around and scramble out of the house, Sara caught them and shouted, "Freeze! You two are going nowhere. We have a wedding to finish planning." She led them into the kitchen and made them sit at the table. "Here's the guest list. I made your moms cut down on the number of people. We're currently down to one hundred. Please add the important guests you want to include. Try to keep it under thirty."

Ken smiled and sweetly said, "Sara, you're my hero."

"Yeah, yeah, get busy. When you finish, please give it to Jesse so he can add his guests. And don't take all day. We have a lot more to cover today."

They finished and handed the list to Sara, who carefully scrutinized it. "Wait, there's only one set of grandparents on the list. They all live right here in town."

Ken looked at the mothers and said, "Are you two kidding me? Grandparents come first. Eliminate your old neighbor's best friend's dog."

Sara panicked. "There's a dog on the guest list?"

Ken laughed at her. "No, it was an exaggeration. Mom and Janie, take off and add."

The women debated back and forth but took off a few and added the rest of their parents, grandparents, and in-laws.

Sara took the list and stated, "Under penalty of death, don't sneak another soul onto the list. Bob and Carrie Ann are emailing or texting everyone they can and will send out written invites to the others."

"Wow, that is so nice of them," Ken said, smiling.

Sara smugly replied, "Not so nice. You and Jesse are going to do their invitations in return."

Jesse flatly said, "Not me, I'll be busy."

Sara disappeared for a second and returned with a rolling pin. "Excuse me, what did you just say?"

Jesse's eyes blew wide open. "I said I'd be glad to help."

Sara handed them the venue, caterers, and florist invoices. The cost was listed on each invoice. The venue was at St. Michael's Wedding Venue, an old church converted into a beautiful wedding hall. The caterers would serve finger food. She planned for the wedding to start in the early afternoon. No alcohol, only fruit punch and sodas. Flowers for the tables and at the wedding vow area only. Sara pointed to the flower invoice. "That's only if neither of you plans on carrying a wedding bouquet."

Ken and Jesse frowned and said simultaneously, "Not funny."

Sara laughed and pointed at the faces they made. "The entire wedding will cost four thousand six hundred and fifty-seven dollars."

Ken and Jesse gaped at her.

"What? I don't think it can be done for much less," Sara said.

Barry and Paul had joined the group. Paul said, "That's it? Really? Barry and I figured at least double that."

Nanette shook her head. "You all missed a pro at work. That girl can wheel and deal. I've never seen anything like it.

The first time, she said *Are you kidding me? Do better than that, or I'll find someone who will. It's Dr. Hanover and Dr. Van Dever's wedding, after all.* And when the venue manager dropped the price in half, I about had a stroke. She just bowled everyone over after that. Sara, honey, you need to do this for a living or at least a side job."

Sara smiled. Ken stood and looked at her. She locked gazes with him. Ken's eyes pooled with tears first, and then Sara followed suit. "Sara, how will I ever thank you?"

"I'm forgiven then?" Her eyes moved from Ken to Jesse.

Both men got up and hugged her. The room had only quiet sniffles. "Absolutely forgiven," Jesse said.

Sara stepped back and told them, "Now, we're going shopping for your wedding outfits."

Vlad interrupted, "You certainly are not. You're going home and putting your feet up and resting. Ken and Jesse are bringing you your favorite Chinese for supper. No discussion. Let's go."

As Vlad led her out, she paused. "You two, it's a formal affair, no camping, cowboy, redneck, or casual attire. You both need to go and get tuxes *today*."

Ken waved. "Goodbye, Sara. We'll see you in a couple of hours."

Ken and Jesse sat down, and Ken said, "I'm glad that's done. I think Jesse and I need a nap."

Their mothers looked at each other and then at their sons. "Tuxes and right now," they simultaneously scolded. Ken and Jesse saw clearly that their mothers meant business. They quickly got up and fled the house.

Ken felt overwhelmed. Shopping for wedding tuxedos was not as easy as the two of them thought it would be. First of all, there were thousands of different tuxes.

After about fifteen minutes of looking, Jesse got totally goofy. "Okay, Ken, let's each secretly pick out a fun tux. Go try it on and surprise each other. Then we'll snap a picture and send it to Sara for approval."

The two of them took off, picked their choices, and dressed. Jesse told Ken through the dressing room curtain, "On the count of three, we both step out. Ready? One, two, three."

Out they stepped. They took one look at each other and fell out laughing. Jesse had a lavender velvet tux with red trim. Ken had a rust-colored one with black trim.

"Hurry and take the pic and send it," Jesse said. "She's going to just shit."

Immediately, Ken's phone blew up. "Hello, what do you think?" he put his phone on speaker.

"I think you both did a wonderful job. Now, go down to the barber and get your heads shaved. Nothing else would possibly do."

Jesse had a frightened expression. "Okay, we'll send the real ones in fifteen minutes."

"Oh, darn, those aren't your actual choices."

Ken grumbled, "I hate it when she does that."

Jesse nodded in agreement.

They picked beautiful morning tuxedos. Black blazer and gray pants. They both looked so damn handsome. The tuxes needed some tailoring to fit perfectly. The tailor measured their arms, shoulders, waist, and hips. Then he knelt down to measure the inseams. Jesse started to get uncomfortable. "You'll have to let Ken do it for you. There is no way I'm going to let anyone get that personal with my junk. You've already been too handsy for my liking."

Ken bristled and said, "Handsy, how handsy?"

Jesse grimaced. "He's too touchy and squeezed my butt cheek?"

The tailor feigned shock.

"Get your boss here, now." Ken sounded very assertive.

The store owner arrived. Jesse told him. "I don't feel

comfortable. I want my fiancé to measure my inseam. Your tailor is too handsy for my liking."

"Sir, I'll do it myself."

"No." Jesse shook his head.

"But, sir, your fiancé had this done without issue."

"Ken is the only one who ever touched or is ever going to touch my junk." Jesse's face started to get red, and he looked angry.

The store owner handed the tape measure to Ken. "Start at the top, a little higher." Ken's eyes widened, giving Jesse a quick, shocked look. The owner continued, "That's it. Now, measure down to his shoe. That's it. Thank you."

Jesse told Ken, "I told you somebody would be touching my junk."

Ken winked at the store owner. "Now you know why I'm marrying him."

The store owner laughed. "You can pick them up on Monday. Thank you for your business."

They left the shop and walked down the street. They stopped for a couple of to-go coffees at the local coffee shop and continued down the street. "Why are you commando today?" Ken asked with one raised eyebrow, looking puzzled at Jesse.

"I didn't bring enough underwear."

"Jesse, you're hung like a horse. Underwear for you is like a bra for a big-boobed woman, a necessity!"

Jesse spat his coffee and started laughing. He couldn't seem to stop.

"I'm going to tell your mom and sister. And if anyone finds out you tried on pants without underwear, oh my."

"Ken, if you do that, I'll never forgive you. I mean it. Don't make me cry," Jesse pleaded.

"Fine, we're going to the department store and buying you fifty pairs of underwear."

They did stop, but Jesse decided ten pairs was more than enough. As they walked out of the store, Ken said, "I don't want you sharing your junk with others. It's mine and mine alone, well, and yours, too, of course."

"You want to know something?"

"What?"

"I kinda like the feeling of the commando stuff."

Ken laughed. "Shut up. You really are just a big teenager, aren't you?"

"Big, yes. Teenager, no."

They stopped at the local jewelry store and bought gold bracelets for their mothers, Carrie Ann, and Sara. They also got gold key rings for the fathers, Bob, and Vlad. Walking out of the shop, Jesse said, "We spent more on these gifts than what our parents will spend on the wedding. Not quite, but it's worth it. You were right to get the same for everyone. Now, when any of them see one, it'll remind them of our special day." Ken started to tear up. Jesse saw the watery eyes and pulled Ken into a bear hug.

CHAPTER NINE

Sara made Jesse and Ken dress in separate areas of the venue. "It's just bad luck." She walked into Ken's dressing room and found him sobbing. She glanced down the hall and saw Carrie Ann. "Go get Jesse, stat. We have a major melt-down happening." She turned back to Ken. "Sweetheart, what's wrong?" Sara tried to console Ken.

Jesse stormed into the room. "Now, what did you do?" he harshly asked Sara, taking Ken into his arms and pulling him close.

"Jesse, I swear I found him like this. I've no idea why he's so upset."

Ken stepped back. "It's all just so beautiful. I can't believe this fairytale is my life."

Sara gave them both a hug. "Well, it is, so get used to it. Jesse, get to your place. Ken, you totally fucked up your make-up. You have ten minutes. Get moving."

Ten minutes later, the music started. Jesse met Ken at the back of the venue, and they walked down the aisle together. They stopped up front where the justice of the peace awaited them.

The justice of the peace looked at the grooms. "Are you two ready?"

They both nodded.

"We are here to join in marriage Jesse Paul Hanover and Kenneth Bartholomew Van Dever."

Jesse mouthed, "Bartholomew?" A mischievous smile

spread across Jesse's face.

Ken mouthed back, "Mother. Commando."

The justice of the peace asked, "Could you two come back to the program? Now I understand they will say their own vows."

Jesse took both of Ken's hands. "I built this wall around me to keep everyone I loved out, but your love built a wall that took me in and made my wall crumble. I never thought you'd love me like you do. I'm so glad you never gave up on me, even when I gave up on myself. I love you, Kenny. Will you please marry me?"

"Yes, Jesse, I will marry you." Ken's tears of joy rolled down his cheeks.

Jesse placed the ring on Ken's finger. "This is a symbol of my undying love for you."

Ken cleared his throat. "Jesse, you've held my heart in your hands since the first day I met you. I want to share my life with you. Will you grow old with me? Will you walk through life with me? Jesse, will you marry me?"

Jesse sputtered, trying not to cry. He opened his mouth to speak twice, but nothing came out. Finally, he said, "Kenny, I will marry you." Ken slid a gold band on Jesse's finger. "This ring is a symbol of my love. It's a circle, and it has no beginning and no end like my love for you."

"I pronounce them married. You may kiss your groom."

Applause thundered through the former church. The grooms faced the guests, kissed, and smiled at the guests. Cameras flashed. Ken and Jesse walked down the aisle to the reception area. The guest waited until the couple got to the reception area. The grooms wanted to be set to welcome and thank the guests.

As Jesse and Ken walked down the hall ahead of the crowd, Jesse leaned close to Ken and whispered, "I'm commando."

Jesse's words shocked Ken, who looked up at him. "You're

kidding?"

"Nope. I'm actually freeballing it on our wedding day." Jesse started chuckling.

"You'll be sorry."

"Nope. I kinda like this feeling."

Ken grabbed Jesse and quickly pulled him into an alcove. He kissed him passionately and then reached down and grabbed his crotch. "Now, let's go to the reception."

"Ken, I promise you, I'll get even."

Red-faced Jesse readjusted himself and followed Ken to the reception.

The guests all followed. There was finger food and sodas for refreshments. Ken led a perplexed Jesse to the dance floor for their wedding dance. "Ken, what's going on?"

Ken laughed and said, "You silly man, it's our wedding dance."

Jesse looked terrified at Ken. "Ken, I don't know how to dance. I've never even been to a dance."

"Why not?"

Tears welled up in Jesse's eyes. His voice was emotion-filled. "Because I couldn't take you."

Ken wrapped his arms around Jesse's neck and pulled him in tight. "Oh Jesse, it's okay. Put your arms around my waist and follow what I do."

The first few moments were awkward. Jesse stepped on Ken's toes. He apologized over and over.

Ken quietly said, "Jesse, look at me. Now feel what my body does." That worked, at least well enough for them to pull it off for the dance. The music stopped, and the guests applauded. Jesse leaned down and kissed Ken.

"Again, you saved me," he whispered in Ken's ear. "I love you so damned much."

People mingled and danced. All in all, it was truly a fairytale come true.

CHAPTER TEN

Four months later, Jesse happened to be the one on OB call. He and Ken were at home dining when the call came in. Jesse answered, "Hello, Dr. Hanover."

"Dr. Hanover, this is Delores in the ER. We need you here, STAT. Mrs. Sarcoff is in labor. She and the baby are struggling."

"You'll have to get Dr. Swenson or Dr. Martin. She's family, and it would be unethical for me to treat her."

"Doctor, you're the only one in town able to help. Swenson is at his father's funeral in Wisconsin, and Martin is here in the hospital with a fractured femur. So you're the only one available. That overrides any relationship issues. Get here now."

Jesse hung up and turned to Ken. "It's Sara. She's struggling, and so is the baby. I'm the only doctor available."

"Jesse, get your stuff, and I'll pull out the car. Don't give me that look. I'm coming with you. Sara's going to need everyone there for her."

They dashed to the car and took off. Jesse held on for dear life as Ken shot past a patrol car speeding too fast. The blue lights flashed. Ken didn't pull over.

Jesse said, "Ken, have you gone crazy? Pull over. Now."

Ken whipped the car into the ER entry and stopped. Jesse got out, flashed his ID, and ran into the building.

Police officers carefully walked up to the driver's side window. Ken rolled down the window. "Sorry, I couldn't stop.

My husband, Dr. Hanover, had a delivery emergency."

"Ken Van Dever? Is that you?"

"Yep, but it's Ken Hanover now. Greg? It's Sara. She and the baby are in trouble."

"Vlad's Sara?"

"Yes."

"What the hell. Park the car and get the hell in there."

Ken rushed into the ER. He stopped at the desk. "Sara Sarcoff is here having her baby. Where do I go?"

"Sir, I need your name, and I'll have to check to see if you're on the list."

Ken gave his name and then waited patiently for her to check.

Jesse rushed to labor and delivery. Vlad met him at the door to Sara's room. "Jesse, she's in trouble. We never told anyone, but she's having twins. The nurse says both she and the babies are having a rough time."

Jesse patted Vlad on the shoulder and walked into the room. "Well, Sara, it seems you're full of surprises here. Tell me, how are you feeling." Jesse checked her chart and the monitors as he spoke to her.

"Jesse, I'm so fricking scared. Are the babies okay? My blood pressure is way too high."

"Honey, the twin's heart rate drops with every contraction. That, in itself, isn't too bad, but your blood pressure is way up there, and looking at this ultrasound, the babies are wrapped around each other. Sweet lady, I think we need to do an emergency c-section. Okay?"

Sara's eyes widen with fear. "Jesse, please don't let anything happen to my babies. Where in the hell is Ken? I need Ken."

Jesse turned to the nurse. "Is the OR prepped and ready?

Can you go get Ken? Sara needs him right now."

Jesse looked at the medical staff. "We need to get rolling here. Stat." The team disconnected the wires from the machines and readied Sara for transfer.

Ken rushed into the room, took one look at an extremely pale Vlad, and hugged him. "It's going to be all right." He moved to Sara and squeezed her hand. "Girl, I'm here for you, Vlad, and the baby."

Sara, Vlad, and Jesse said simultaneously. "Babies."

Ken's eyes nearly bugged out of his head. "You sneak! Twins?"

Jesse suddenly interrupted, "We got to go right now." The staff rushed Sara out and down to the OR.

Jesse stopped, hugged Vlad, and said, "She's a tough one. She'll get through this. See you in a little while."

Ken and Vlad sat in the waiting area outside of the Obstetric OR. They alternated sitting and pacing. One hour after they had taken Sara in, Jesse came out. He looked incredibly concerned and tired.

Jesse sat them down and spoke to Vlad. "Vlad, the babies are two identical boys and are struggling a bit. Their umbilical cords were wrapped around everywhere. I'll take you to them in just a minute."

"Sara? How's my Sara?" Vlad asked.

"Vlad, she had a hard time of it. She went into cardiac arrest, but we brought her back. She lost some blood. Vlad, she's critical."

"I must go to her. Please take me." Vlad's hands shook, and he looked so frightened.

Jesse told Ken, "I'll be back as soon as possible."

Ken nodded and then cried when they left.

"Vlad, she's awake but exhausted and weak. There are your sons. They look better already. Aren't they beautiful?" Jesse said gently.

Vlad watched for just a second as the staff cleaned them and applied oxygen to them. He kissed each of his sons' heads and moved to Sara. "Sara, love, you did a wonderful job. The boys are just perfect. They're good-looking like their daddy." Sara smiled weakly. Vlad took her hand and kissed it.

Sara sounded so frail as she spoke to Vlad. "Did they tell you I had some problems? I love you, Vlad Sarcoff. If I don't make it, take care of our boys. Jesse and Ken will be there to help you." She smiled lovingly at Vlad. She winced and said, "Jesse, something is wrong."

The monitor went crazy. Sara arched her back and screamed in pain. Then she became silent.

Vlad looked at Jesse. Jesse moved Vlad away, and the staff crowded around her.

"Clear." Sara's body reacted. "She's back. We have a heartbeat." Jesse then started barking orders, "We need cardiology, stat. Her blood pressure is low. Check her blood count and tell ICU we are on our way."

They flew down the hall to the ICU. Ken caught up with Vlad and ran with him. The ICU staff immediately took over. Vlad stood holding her hand and telling her how much he loved her.

Ken stood out of the way. Jesse glanced at his husband, and their eyes met and locked, each questioning the other. Jesse sadly shook his head and mouthed, "I'm sorry."

The heart specialist and ICU doctors had taken over. Dr. Jenny Gray asked to speak with Jesse out of the room. "Dr. Hanover, why wasn't I called immediately when Mrs. Sarcoff went into labor? I should have been there to monitor her heart."

"Dr. Gray, I read Sara's complete medical history before we did the c-section. There was not one word about any heart issues, and Sara never said a word about it either."

"That's not possible." She marched over to the nearest computer and indicated for Jesse to log in.

As Jesse logged in, he asked her, "Why didn't you log in to Sara's records?"

"We're on a different system as we only have rights here and are not entitled to computer access yet. I emailed Dr. Swenson a very detailed report and all the test results five months ago. The records have to be here."

Jesse stepped back and let her go through Sara's records.

She nearly screeched, "Are you fucking kidding me. The lazy fuck didn't enter anything I sent. Here, let me show you." She opened her laptop and pulled up her email account. She showed Jesse all the information she'd sent Dr. Swenson. He even acknowledged he received them.

"Holy shit." Jesse picked up the phone. "Amy, I need you to find Dr. Swenson. It's an emergency. Send him to my cell. Thanks."

One of the staff stepped out. "Dr. Gray. You are needed, now."

Suddenly both Vlad and Ken were pressed up against Jesse's chest, sobbing. He patted them and just let them cry. After a few minutes, Jesse asked Vlad, "Did you know about Sara's heart condition?"

"Yes, I learned about it a couple of months ago. She didn't want anyone to know. She told me Dr. Gray told her it would be best to terminate the pregnancy, so she kept it a secret until it was too late. Jesse, I swear I had no idea how serious it was. Sara made me believe it was nothing to worry about. Jesse, is she going to make it?"

"The c-section went like clockwork, and everything looked great. Then she had a cardiac arrest, and it went downhill. Dr.

Gray is the best. We'll have to pray she can work her magic."

Ken squeezed Jesse's hand. "How did this happen? Why didn't Dr. Gray show up when she was in labor?"

"Ken, you know I can't tell you that, but we're working on what went wrong."

Jesse's cell phone buzzed, and he stepped away and answered it, "Hello."

"Dr. Hanover, I have Mrs. Swenson, his mother, on the line. You really need to talk with her."

"Hello, Mrs. Swenson, This is Dr. Jesse Hanover. I'm so very sorry for your loss."

"What loss?"

"Your husband? Ronald told us he needed leave to attend his father's funeral."

"My husband is fishing off our dock as I speak. What's Ronald up to now?"

"I'm so sorry, but do you know where he is?"

Mrs. Swenson's voice deepened and sounded angry. "He's at a medical conference in Hawaii. According to him, you made him go."

"Mrs. Swenson, there's no medical conference in Hawaii."

"Dr. Hanover, I promise he will be calling you very soon." She hung up.

A few moments later, Jesse's phone pinged. He had a text message.

Swenson — *This better be important. You do know I'm at my father's funeral, right?*

Jesse — *Liar. I just got off the phone with your mother. You're in Hawaii.*

Swenson — *Why in the hell did you call my folks?*

Jesse — *Sara Sarcoff. Call me now!*

Jesse's phone rang. "Hello."

"What's up with Sara Sarcoff? She's not due for two weeks."

"Are you on your computer looking at her file?"

"Yep, so what's the big emergency?"

"She had to have an emergency c-section. She was in trouble when I arrived here. We reviewed her records, but there was no information about any heart issues. She went into cardiac arrest during the c-section. We called in Dr. Gray. She showed me the complete records she sent you. You never entered them."

"Wait, wait, wait. Yes, I did. I'm sure I did."

"Roger, you're looking at her file, right? Where are they in that file?"

"Shit, come on, Jesse. I made a mistake."

"You, Dr. Gray, and Sara are the only ones who knew the seriousness of her condition. She didn't even tell her husband. Your mistake may cost her life. You get your lying ass back here ASAP. FYI, you're fired." Jesse hung up.

Dr. Gray joined Jesse, Ken, and Vlad. The three men looked at her, terrified. She quickly said, "We've got her stabilized for now. I don't know how much damage has occurred due to the cardiac arrests. She needs open heart surgery. Mr. Sarcoff, your wife has a defect with her heart. It needed to be repaired years ago. But now it's imperative that we do it immediately. With her current condition, it will be very risky, at best. Without the surgery, she won't make it."

Vlad cried as he spoke, "I don't know what to do. Why didn't she tell me about this? Jesse, Ken, please help me. I don't want to lose her."

Jesse and Ken hugged him. Jesse said, "Dr. Gray is the best cardiac specialist in this state, maybe in the country. I trust her word and believe she's our only hope. Now go and be with Sara."

Vlad turned to go, but he first nodded to Dr. Gray and left to be with Sara.

Dr. Gray told the staff to prep Sara for surgery. She looked at Jesse. "Will you scrub up and be in there with the team, please?" Jesse agreed, and She hurried off.

"Ken, call our moms and tell them what's happening. They need to come and take care of Sara's babies. I love you, Ken. Pray hard."

"Is this going to work?" Ken asked.

"It's our only hope." Jesse kissed him and rushed toward the OR.

Six hours later, Ken sat with Vlad in the waiting room. Ken and Jesse's fathers sat with them. The four men cried, paced, and prayed together.

Ken told his friend, "Vlad, I called our moms, and they're caring for the babies here in the nursery. They're doing great."

Vlad looked at Ken. Tears started rolling again. "Good God, I forgot about the boys. Thank you for taking care of them and me."

Ken heard Jesse's excited voice coming toward the waiting room. Jesse and Dr. Gray bust through the double doors. Jesse exclaimed, "This woman is a miracle worker."

Dr. Gray smiled and then said, "The operation was a success. Sara is in very stable condition. I believe she'll have a full recovery. I was able to do keyhole surgery, so Sara's recovery will happen quickly." She shook her finger at Vlad. "No more babies, at least none until we're sure she can do it without risk."

Vlad hugged her and said, "Thank you, thank you so much. When can I see her?"

"I'll take you to her right now." Off they went.

Ken sat, covered his face, and sobbed. His and Jesse's fathers move to comfort him. "No, I got this. Please go check on the moms and the babies." They smiled and left.

Ken needed Jesse. He wrapped his arms around Jesse's neck and cried. "I'm just so happy she's alive," he said into

Jesse's chest. He sat up, wiped his tears, frowned deeply, and said, "When she gets better, I'm going to kill her. What the hell was she thinking? I'm just so mad at her."

"Well, if you're going to kill her, why did we do the surgery?" Jesse teased.

Ken angrily said, "Shut up, you know what I meant. Her damn stubbornness nearly killed her. I just want to choke her out. Snatch her bald-headed. Beat her with a stick and hug her neck."

Jesse laughed at him. "Ah, Ken, are you wiping snot on my scrubs? Okay, I get it, you're mad at her. Just make sure Dr. Gray okays it before you do anything."

"Can I see her?"

"Not until they move her to the ICU. She's in recovery now. She'll be in the hospital for a while."

Sara, the Director of Nursing, proved to be the worst patient. She demanded, bitched, yelled, and ordered the nursing staff around. Jesse had to yell at her. "Sara, I swear I'll have you restrained and gagged if you abuse one more person on this staff."

The nursing staff threw a party the moment Sara left the hospital.

A couple of weeks later, Jesse and Ken brought over a very fancy dinner and lots of stuff for the babies. Sara wanted company. She was nearly back to her old self. Vlad reminded her to be nice.

"I was not that bad. Jesse's exaggerating."

Jesse gaped at her for a second. "They threw a party the second you left the hospital. Some of them cried because they were so happy."

Sara made an uh-no face. "Crap, I'm going to have to do some major apologizing to do when I go back to work. I hate apologizing."

The three men simultaneously said, "We know."

Jesse added. "I'd bring gifts. Expensive gifts."

Chapter Eleven

Ken and Jesse planned to celebrate their third anniversary on a cruise ship, but that didn't work out. "Jesse, Jesse," Ken called, all excited.

"What's up, Doc?" Jesse walked into Ken's home office and leaned his hands on the desk.

"Jesse." Ken's emotions welled up to the point he couldn't speak.

"Honey, what's wrong? Tell me."

"Andy."

"Don't tell me those shit parents changed their mind. For fuck sake, they threw that poor baby away years ago."

"He's ours. The adoption went through. We go before the judge tomorrow."

Jesse danced around the room. "We need to tell Andy."

"Wait, there's more. Wendy's pregnant. Eight weeks."

"Our Wendy?" Jesse asked in disbelief.

"We definitely picked the right surrogate. First time, and it took."

"Do you want to know which one of us is going to be the dad and which one of us is going to be the mom?" Ken teased.

Jesse pinched Ken's butt. "Tell me."

"Very funny, asshole. You're the bio, and I'm the real. She didn't know which sample they randomly picked until today. Now let's go tell Andy. He's watching television in our bedroom."

They entered the bedroom. Andy's eyes got big. He looked so frightened. Ken rushed to him. "We've good news."

Jesse chimed in excitedly. "We have *great* news."

Andy climbed into Ken's lap. "Sweet Andy, tomorrow we go before the judge. You'll be forever our son."

Andy looked back and forth between his dads. "For real?"

Ken and Jesse both said, "For real!"

Andy jumped off the bed and went running and screaming through the house. He returned and hugged them both.

Ken patted the bed for Andy to sit. "There's something else. You're going to be a big brother in about seven months from now."

Andy counted off the months. "January, February, March, April, May, June, July." His entire face lit up. "July. That's my birthday month. Maybe my baby will be born on my birthday. Jess and Ken, from now on, Ken will be Dad A, and Jesse will be Dad B."

Ken raised his eyebrows. "One of us could be just Dad and the other Papa or Daddy."

Andy stared at him without expression. "No. Dad A and Dad B."

Jesse said to Ken, "Looks like that's final."

Christmas exploded with celebrations. Andy got two dads, two sets of grandparents, an aunt and uncle, cousins, and many other relatives. His excitement lit up the room. Ken and Jesse let Andy make the announcement about the baby to their parents. Jesse and Ken's moms whooped it up and hugged everyone.

Janie happily said, "That makes three babies coming in July."

Jesse looked confused and then saw the same confusion on Ken's face. "Mom, what are you talking about?"

Janie flushed with embarrassment. "Oops. I have a big mouth. Oh well, the cat's out of the bag now. Bob and Carrie Ann are having their second, and Vlad and Sara are also expecting."

Jesse grabbed Ken's hand. They both looked at Sara, stunned. Jesse finally spoke, "Are you going to be okay? Did Dr. Grey tell you it was safe to do this again?"

Sara took Jesse's hands first and then Ken's. "Boys, I'd never do anything to risk my life again. I've two little guys and a husband to take care of. Besides, Dr. Grey readily approved this. So stop worrying. Vlad is worrying enough for everyone."

The Christmas celebration continued. The spirit of Christmas filled the house.

Paul raised his glass and toasted, "To our ever-growing family."

The room filled with *Hear, Hear!*

The toasts of love went around the room. Sara raised her glass of apple juice. "Seeing I'm the last to toast. Here's to support bras used by well-endowed women." Pointing to herself. "And to jockey shorts for overly endowed men. Take the hint, Jesse."

Jesse spat out his wine and glared at Sara, who just shrugged.

Ken barked out the loudest laugh and then rolled back and forth on the sofa laughing so hard he cried.

Jesse's mom asked, "Jesse, what's this all about?"

Jesse blushed. "Nothing. It's just Sara being mean to me." Stepping behind where Ken sat on the sofa, he said, "Ken, you need to stop."

Ken reached backward and tweaked Jesse's member. "Told you."

Laughter filled the room. Everyone laughed at Jesse's expense.

He leaned down and whispered in Ken's ear. "You better run."

Ken took one look at Jesse's expression and took off

through the living room and down the hall.

Jesse caught him, picked him up, and threw him on the nearest bed. He pounced and held Ken down. "Why did you tell Sara that?" he asked as he tickled Ken.

"I swear I never did that," Ken said between tickles.

Jesse stopped. "Then how did she know?"

"Duh, Jesse. I've told you before. You're too big not to be noticed. It's as big around as my arm and hangs nearly to your knee. Hard to miss, don't you think?"

Jesse smirked. "You never complained."

"You're right. But I never imagined you'd put it on display, either."

Jesse's eyes widened with surprise. "Is that what you think? That isn't true. I just like the feeling of hanging free."

Ken grabbed his face and pulled him into a kiss. "Time for us to go home."

"Not yet. Our son still gets to open his presents from his family. I want to be around when he does it."

Andy carefully opened his presents one at a time. He carefully unwrapped the paper so it wouldn't tear. He took time to look each over and thank the person who gave it to him. It took forever.

Jesse's turn came. "Andy, watch and learn." He ripped off the paper, looked at the gift, and thanked the giver. "That, my son, is how it's done."

Andy flatly said, "You don't seem very appreciative if you ask me."

Laughter filled the room as Jesse pounced on Andy and tickled him.

EPILOGUE

Jesse, Ken, and Andy counted the months, days, and then hours. Finally July arrived, and the babies came. Jesse left the delivery room and announced, "Sara and Vlad's baby boy came, and all was well. Mom and baby are healthy. Sara told me to tell you *Looks like I'm destined to have boys.*"

Jesse's team kept busy. Next, Carrie Ann and Bob's babies arrived one week later. It wasn't a secret that they were having twins. The boys were born via c-section. Carrie Ann cried a little as she really wanted girls. But now she had three boys, just like Sara.

Two weeks later, Andy woke up Jesse and Ken. "Dad A and Dad B, it's time to get up. My baby's being born."

Jesse looked at him like he was crazy. "Son, you don't get to decide this." At that moment, the phone rang. Jesse picked it up. "Hello. It's three-twenty in the morning."

"Jesse, it's Wendy."

Jesse put the phone on speaker. "Wendy? What's up?"

"That's a stupid question. Why the hell else would I call you guys in the middle of the night? I'm having your baby. If you want to be here, you better haul ass. This is going way faster than anyone thought it would. You have about fifteen minutes. Got to go. Contraction."

Jesse, Ken, and Andy made it just in time to see Jessica Kendra Hanover enter the world. She came out screaming mad. She squalled the entire time they cleaned her up. The nurse brought her to Wendy, who only kissed her little crying face. "Take her to her parents and brother."

Still screaming, Baby Jessica stopped the second the nurse put her in Andy's lap and waiting arms. Andy started crying. He looked up and Jesse and Ken. "She loves me. Now I have a whole family that loves me." Jesse stood teary-eyed. He walked up behind Ken and wrapped his arms around him. He said, "You're loved by everyone that knows you."

He kissed Ken on the neck. Ken suddenly stiffened, turned his head, and whispered harshly, "Commando? Are you kidding me? Oh my God, those sweats are so thin you can tell that you're circumcised."

Jesse laughed. "I was in a hurry. Besides, I sort of like it. I think I might be a nudist at heart."

"I know what you like. You better stop rubbing up against me before the world knows."

"I love you, Kenny."

"Me, too."

ABOUT THE AUTHOR

I am a retired educator, and I live with my teenage son and our very elderly Papa. We live on a beautiful farm in the northeast Georgia Mountains. I spend time writing and tending the many animals on the farm.

www.ingramcontent.com/pod-product-compliance
Lightning Source LLC
Chambersburg PA
CBHW070538130626
46555CB00003B/1480